Dancing

Without

Music

Books by Angela Grey

Spirit Pass: A Jessica Stone Novella #1
Missing and Murdered Indigenous Women & Girls: A Jessica Stone Novella #2
The Lasting Echo of Lost Souls: A Jessica Stone Novella #3
Resilience Throughout Recovery
Beyond Quirky
Run Fast, Run Far
Sifting Through a Storied Past
Coteau des Prairies Runaway
Prologue to an Epitaph
A Childhood Lost to the Wind
Déjà vu
Of Laughter & Heartbreak
Beating Drum of a Broken Heart
Nostalgic Tendencies, Idyllic Endeavors & Current Inclinations
Between Shadows and Lies
Bedridden & Gutted to Mindful
Bdote
Dreamcatcher
The Cartography of First Love
Whimsy and Bliss

Also by Angela Grey & Paige Peterson

Lake of Secrets
Dancing Without Music
Echoes of the Past
Echoes at Midnight
Madness and Mayhem
Long Since Buried
Since You've Been Gone
Some Species of Outsider-ness

Dancing Without Music

ANGELA GREY

PAIGE PETERSON

To the love of my life, Robert,
and our four adult children,
Paige, Cody, Chase, & Brooke,
children-in-law
Vince and Angel,
and grandsons Logan and Luke

—AG

CONTENTS

COVER

ALSO BY THIS AUTHOR

TITLE PAGE

COPYRIGHT

DEDICATION

CONTENTS

ACKNOWLEDGMENTS

ACKNOWLEDGMENTS

Thank you to my Twitter beta readers
and Goodreads reviewers. Your ongoing suggestions
and advice are tremendously helpful and appreciated.

Mia

ACES AND EIGHTS
(DEAD MAN'S HAND)

Hi. I'm seventeen-year-old Mia Callan, a kid of fortunate circumstances, I guess, but why don't I feel like it? There's my dad, Seth Callan, and Mom, Sara. I also have a little brother, Ben. We're like four peas in a pod with appearances: petite, dark-haired, matching eyes, and olive complexions.

I'm homeschooled by my piano teacher-dad and freelance writer-mom, as is Ben, who is twelve. Violet Morgan, petite but with a feisty persona for her frame, is my only friend. She occupies any room that she enters. She's a piano student of my dad's, which is how we met eleven years ago. Our favorite thing to do is work out. My dad worries we do it too much: elliptical, treadmill, rower, exercise bike, interactive, global, and trainer-led workouts via online videos in my basement. It was supposed to be my mom's exercise studio, but I took it over from the get-go, as mom says. Plus, Violet and I run, hike, and bike on the trails surrounding our suburb and interconnected throughout the city.

My mom teaches my brother and me throughout the morning and gives us assignments in the afternoon when she catches up on her writing. My dad sees piano students from 8:00 am to 8:00 pm in the front parlor. Most of his day, he teaches homeschooled kids, and the evening focuses on those who attend the district schools, like twins Rory and his sister Kira, who are incredibly attractive and are two years younger than me.

I often wonder what life is like for two perfect-looking teens, like Rory and Kira. I bet they have tons of friends, unlike me. They're probably 4.0 GPA students, also unlike me, and with tons of extracurricular activities. I bet she's a cheerleader or on the dance team, and he's a football or soccer player. The world is their oyster.

Their house is probably gorgeous, unlike ours. We live in a cookie-cutter suburban two-story bungalow where our front-facing dining room was turned into a parlor. The baby grand is in the window with a loveseat and my dad's desk taking up the rest of that space. That leaves our family to dine in our built-in breakfast nook or at the island countertop. The other front-facing room is the living room, where I usually spend my afternoon assignment sessions, as I am now, completing what's expected of me while I people-watch all my dad's clients and wonder what their lives are like compared to mine. Comparison for me is like the sword of Damocles.

When sibling clients or moms or dads accompany the piano student, they usually sit in the living room with me while they wait. It's never usually awkward unless a cute guy, like this one walking up the walkway with what must be his younger brother, attends my dad's lessons.

Lessons begin after Labor Day, like today, or after New Year's Day, after Easter, and again at the beginning of June. Mom rushes to the door to greet the new students.

"Hello, come inside. I'm Sara Callan. My husband, Seth, is in with a student. They should finish up soon. Please take a seat in our living room here with my daughter Mia." Mom shows them the stone-colored sectional sofa across from where I'm reading in the taupe leather rocker-recliner.

"Thank you. I'm Milo Chatham, and this is my little brother, Beckett," the brown-haired, tall, handsome teenager with striking brown eyes says. His little brother puts his hand out for my mom to shake.

"Such perfect gentlemen," Mom replies as my brother enters the room. "Oh, and this is my son, Ben. Both my kids are homeschooled. I hope you don't mind, but they do their reading in here in the afternoons."

"Not at all," Milo says upon glancing at me a few moments too long.

I think my face just flushed. Hopefully, nobody noticed. Mom rushes into the kitchen when her phone rings.

"I'm done reading. Do you want to play some cards?" Ben asks Beckett and Milo. "Mia, you can play, too."

"You mean like Go Fish?" Beckett wonders.

"No, like poker. My grandma taught me this past weekend," Ben beams.

"Your sister has a beautiful name: Mia," Milo states as his eyes meet mine and linger.

The three boys practice a few games, all of which

Ben wins. In the last game, Ben winces when Milo reveals his unlucky hand just as Dad opens up the door to the piano studio.

"Thank you, Mr. Callan," Wyatt Marsden tells my dad. "Hey, Milo, how's it going?"

"Good, Wyatt. See you in school. Hello, Mr. Callan. This is my brother, Beckett Chatham. He'd like me to go first, if that's okay?"

"Whichever you prefer, boys." Dad gestures Milo into the studio and to the piano.

Meanwhile, Ben and Beckett continue to play cards. It's not quite twenty minutes into the forty-five-minute lesson when a heavy noise, like something big fell, resonates from the piano studio.

"Dad?" both Ben and I yell.

"Sara?" Dad yells from behind the closed door. "Call 911."

Ben, Beckett, and I reach the door simultaneously as Mom dialed on her cell. Milo collapsed onto the floor from where he sat on the piano bench. Mom rushes to gather clean towels from the kitchen to press against his bloody head wound. Dad pushes the furniture out of the way so Milo doesn't hurt himself anymore while his body jerks violently. Afterward, Dad rustles a silent, bloody Milo a good five minutes back to consciousness.

"He stiffened, then groaned, mumbled something, then closed his eyes, and just fell, headfirst, onto the floor and began jerking violently. He's got a blue tinge to him now, but he's breathing. He's also lost control of his bladder. I didn't know how long the seizure was going to last. And he's got that head wound. What do I do?" Dad, who's squeamish, says, turning away from the blood. "Oh, no, I'd better call their mother. You guys take Beckett into the other room while we wait for the ambulance."

Beckett wipes tears from his eyes while Dad talks on the phone with Mrs. Chatham. "I don't know what happened. Milo just stammered, stiffened, then collapsed to the side, headfirst. Yes. We've called an ambulance, and they're on their way. Yes. Beckett is fine. He's right here."

The ambulance arrives and leaves before Mrs. Chatham returns. Beckett runs out to greet her, and Dad follows shortly. I sit on the front stoop and eavesdrop on their conversation.

"I'm so sorry for the commotion. Milo's on a new medication for his seizures, and it's been making him a little depressed and dizzy. Add to that his insomnia and lack of appetite. He just hasn't been himself. We'll be on our way to the hospital. When I get more information, I'll let you know. I'm sorry about this on our first day of lessons," Mrs. Chatham reveals.

"I just hope everything is fine. I'm excited to have the boys back again soon. Take care. I hope everything is well," Dad sympathizes.

Hmm. Milo has epilepsy and depression. He doesn't look depressed. And I should know since I've been depressed for years and look the part. Perhaps that's why I only have one friend. I pull out my phone to text her.

Mia: Hey Vi, this cute guy just collapsed here.
Mia: It turns out he's on new meds.
Mia: R U there?
Violet: I'm here. What's his name?
Mia: Milo Chatham, do U know him?
Violet: Cute guy. Loner. Epilepsy or something.

Mia: Don't tell anyone.
Violet: Do I ever?
Mia: I know you're right about my trust issues.
Violet: What time are we going to run today?
Mia: Just give me some time to change.
Violet: I'll be right over.

I rush up to my neat bedroom, full of books and walls full of abstract art bought from local starving artist fairs. Against the wall near the door is my dual monitor and desktop computer, where I often get carried away with ethical hacking. I expose vulnerabilities in software to help local businesses fix security holes before a malevolent hacker finds them. I only have a handful of small business clients in our suburb, mainly independent contractors like a small design-build firm or trade contractors in the building and remodeling industry, or personal services industry like a maid, a dog-walker, and a singer or gig worker.

As I scour my walk-in closet for suitable shorts that don't make my legs look so fat, I think back to the first time I had chubby body insecurities, which was when I was about twelve and trying on clothes at the mall with my mom. I'm pudgier, a bit more so than my dad. Well, to be honest, he isn't really pudgy, just has some meat on his bones. It doesn't help that we're all short. My friend Violet is like me, but skinnier. She's stick thin and can eat anything without worrying about weight gain.

The first time I starved myself was when I was twelve, after the mall incident with my mom. I started by pushing my plate away before I was finished. Then I'd only take a third of what I'd used to serve myself. Next came the headaches. Mom said it was from not consuming enough water and poor nutrition. But it gave me an excuse to turn away the meal altogether. At some point, I had to eat, or they'd commit me for treatment. So, then I started eating a half can of tomato soup with a leaf of lettuce. That was when I'd hide under the covers with blackout curtains. My parents only let me get away with that for so long. I'm one of those lucky ones with a good health insurance policy that covers commitment for an eating disorder. My parents always resort to that threat when my episodes go too long.

As of late, I control my weight through exercise and self-control at the dinner table. It's time-consuming and takes a lot of mental energy to constantly worry about how I can fend off my next meal. Mom messes me up from time to time with the fad diets she wants me to try to eat healthier. There was a South Beach diet, a Mediterranean diet, a Blue Zone diet, an Atkins diet, a raw food diet, a master cleanse, a vegan diet, a paleo diet, a keto diet, and a zone diet.

Due to all the research on those diets, I've gotten my fair share of information on the benefits and downsides of foods, herbs, and supplements. I wonder if Milo knows about skullcap, lily of the valley, burning bush, hydrocotyle, groundcel, mugwort, tree of heaven, and peony, which are supposedly helpful with preventing seizures. Not that I'd ever get up my nerve to speak with him. He'd never be interested in someone like me. Maybe Violet, but not me.

I see Violet crossing the street. I'd better get down there before my parents harass her about being too thin. I swear it's like their hobby to focus on food and looks. I'm a teenager. That's my realm.

"Hey, it's Violet. We're going out for a run. We'll be

back in a couple of hours if that's okay?" I say as I rush to get to the front door. Dad's in with a piano client, and Mom shrugs me off from where she's typing away at her desk off the kitchen towards the mudroom. At least Ben hears me from where he sits in the living room with the next piano student.

Violet and I warm up on my front lawn, then gradually pick up speed prior to the twenty-mile trail that winds through a half dozen of the western suburbs. Much of it is paved, but there are some gravel spots that you don't want to wipe out on.

"So, you like Milo Chatham?" Violet asks.

"He's cute."

"I don't think he has a girlfriend. I can ask his best friend, Wyatt Marsden," Violet offers.

"Wyatt is Milo's best friend?

"Yup," She says as we make our way through the tunnel under the highway that leads to Lake Ann, where parents watch their kids at the unguarded beach on this hot, late summer day. Technically, Fall doesn't arrive until later this month. Labor Day was a scorching ninety-five, but at least the guarded beaches were still open. Things will start to shut down in quick order now. It doesn't help to think that we could be knee-deep in snow in a couple of short months. I'm still hot and sweaty despite the thoughts. Maybe I'm burning off that apple I had for breakfast or that yogurt for lunch.

We take a left and head towards the arboretum and its wooden walking bridge that leads across the marsh to the apple orchards. Sprinting so nobody can call out to us to stop running on the walking path, we make it to the university-run orchard in no time. Then, down the busy cross street to get to the next suburb over, and its sprawling horse farms. Most of those animals aren't meant for the race track. Instead, city dwellers shelter their horses throughout the countryside and visit as much as they can. Other than that, a few equine therapy farms around are pretty busy up until the first snowfall.

"Milo's mom said he's depressed," I throw out there.

"I believe it," Violet replies.

"What do you mean? Do you believe that I'm depressed? Can you tell?"

"Milo is moody and brooding," Vi explains.

"I didn't get that vibe from him."

"Perhaps he didn't want you to see it."

"And me?"

Violet looks my way and says, "You can't be depressed. Your parents won't let you. They threaten commitment at the drop of a hat when it comes to you."

"That doesn't mean it goes away."

"You should tell them that. Maybe they'll allow you to join a support group and finally get some help for it without committing you to a psych ward," Vi suggests. I come to a complete stop near the archery range and confide, "The sadness about my weight, the anger at my parents, and the confusion as to who I am and who I'm going to be someday don't pass as they tell me it will. Shit, I'm going to be underdeveloped forever."

"I know, sweetie. I know that's why I'm your only friend. You're depressed and want to be alone. It must be a shitload of confusion to have such a lingering sadness and utter despair follow you everywhere like a god damn shadow."

"You know what, Vi. I'm going to tell them I need

to talk to someone about this fucking black cloud hanging over me."

Violet reaches out to hug me. "Everything will work out for you. I think that your parents are your greatest obstacle. Once you get through to them, the barriers will come tumbling down. I think that they just have such high hopes for you and put you on a pedestal that you can't live up to for them."

"What do you say to heading back now? I think we've run ten miles. I still want to lift weights before I shower and do some work," I say.

"I wish that I could get by like you, Mia. It sucks being a cashier at a toy store," Vi adds.

"But you get to be around all those cute little babies in strollers and suggest new clothes to their moms."

"Yeah, I hope I get switched to that department permanently, or at least until I graduate, I mean," Vi informs.

"I don't think I ever want to have kids. I wouldn't want to pass the depression down to them."

"They wouldn't necessarily have it as well."

"Kids sense things. I remember when my parents had their affairs when my brother was in a coma after the car accident. I knew what was happening. They didn't have to tell me. If I had kids, they'd sense my moods and know something was up, and I wouldn't lie to them about it like my parents did to me, which just made the depression worse, despite them working things out."

Milo

THE ABERRATION OF STARLIGHT

"Epilepsy runs my house. My parents can't even plan a vacation where they want. It calls the shots."

"Milo, the right medication will change things," my neurologist, Dr. Rafferty, says. "We'll try another one and see the results; however, your depression needs to be controlled as well. And for that, I'm referring you to a psychiatrist, Dr. Henley. He works with a therapist by the name of Jessica Walsh. Their team of mental health professionals will do wonders for you. Give them a shot." He pats me on the back. "Dr. Henley will be in to see you shortly at the end of his rounds. You take care, young man."

"Okay, son, let's go over the specifics of keeping a seizure diary," says the husky male nurse assigned to me during my stay in the teen section of the children's hospital unit. "When, where, who, how, and what."

"I know. Did the seizure have an aura (a feeling or sense to it)? How did I feel before the seizure? How long did each stage last?"

"Did you take anything: any alcohol, drugs, or

prescriptions before the seizure?" the nurse adds. "Ask anyone there with me, the timing, and if I lost consciousness, and how long to regain it."

"Also, note when your last dose of meds was, what time your next one will be, and whether or not you'd forgotten a dose or not," the nurse finishes just as the shrink enters.

"Hello, Mr. Chatham. My name is Dr. Henley. I just passed your neurologist in the hallway. He says you're a star with woodworking. You make a pretty penny with your products."

"Yeah, well, some stars burn out too soon," I reply.

"Only if they're consumed by a black hole. Other stars last thousands of years."

"Well, depression might just be that black hole of which you speak," I banter.

"Then why don't we do something about that?" the shrink suggests.

"I'm going to prescribe an antidepressant. In addition, I'd like you to see a therapist who works with me. Her name is Jessica Walsh. She'll also get you signed up for some group therapy. We have an excellent group of teenagers that meet once a week to deal with the difficult times depression can bring about in our lives," Dr. Henley says.

"How often do I need to see the therapist?" "You'll work with Jessica once a week. Then you'll attend group weekly as well. And you'll see me once a month unless there is a problem and we need to alter the medication, then we'll meet sooner."

Two days into the school year, and I'm already missing school. Just because the only open appointment Jessica Walsh had this week was during the day, which meant:

I'd have to cut class to see her. Apparently, I'm that fucked up.

"Mr. Chatham, can I call you Milo?" Jessica Walsh asks.

"Yes."

"Thank you. And you can call me Jessica," she points to either the business armchair or the loveseat in her office, so I take the chestnut-colored suede seating opposite the floor-to-ceiling windows that look out over the lake. "I understand that you're a woodworker and a perfect one at that, with plenty of clients?"

"My mom always reminds me of that old adage about idle hands making the devil's workshop, so I've always kept busy."

"How true, and it's very beneficial in staving off depression," Jessica adds.

"Well, that hasn't been the case with me. Lately, I've found less and less enjoyment in woodworking."

"And your irritability factor?" she wonders.

"Through the roof."

"Changes in appetite?" Jessica asks.

"What appetite?"

"How about your sleep patterns?" she asks while taking notes a mile a minute on the tablet on her lap.

"I've never been a sound sleeper. Little noises could always wake me. But lately, I can only take brief naps, and I usually end up awake in the middle of the night feeling worthless and guilty."

"Why is that?"

"I feel guilty that my parents fight about me and my care with my fucking epilepsy."

"If you didn't have epilepsy, do you think that things would be better?"

"To some degree."

"Well, I understand that Dr. Rafferty is working on that by experimenting with different medications. You're going to have to give each one time to work."

"I know. But sometimes it seems like I'm running out of time," I say, then wince. What secrets am I giving up? She has that mandate to report if I'm suicidal. I'll end up in the loony bin.

"What do you mean that you're running out of time, Milo?"

"I can't say," I focus on the turkeys out the window.

"Milo, your mother told me that you've made several suicide attempts. We can talk about them."

"Killing myself is tougher than I thought it would be. I've tried, and I don't…die."

"Then you end up with the suicide blues. I've heard about them many times. This isn't new to me, Milo."

"Please fix me. Make me better," I say, clenching my fists and pounding my knees. "And don't just send me off on a psych ward sojourn."

"Together with the medication, our talks will work towards the betterment of your diagnosis: major depressive disorder," Jessica reveals.

"Well, at least it has a name. One can't really fight something when you don't know that it truly exists, and others don't see it, either."

"We all know of your despair. And we see how hard you are truly trying to beat it," Jessica empathizes. "Let's talk about the positives in your life?" she tries to change the subject.

"Like what?"

"How about your friends? Girlfriends? Boyfriends? Or are there any crushes in your life?"

"I did meet this girl. She's pretty and has a beautiful

name: Mia. But that would never come of anything."

"Why not?" Jessica delves.

"Because I was at her house when I had my seizure. And I sort of lost control of my bladder when I was out. I'm sure she must have laughed her ass off at me."

"You don't know that? She may not have noticed."

"My brother, Beckett, was right beside her. He said everyone saw what I did," I punch my knees again.

"Did Beckett say she laughed?"

"Well, no. He said that they were all scared for me, but when it was over, she probably had herself a chuckle with her parents?"

"Her parents were there, too?"

"I was at her house for my first piano lesson with her dad. I've been practicing for years, but it was my first visit with her dad. I left a strong impression."

"I'm sure her parents explained the gravity of the situation, and there wasn't any laughter at your circumstances. Give this girl a shot."

"I don't know. I don't even know if I really care. She just seemed so pretty in the short time I saw her. I wish—"

"What? What do you wish for Milo?"

"I wish that I could have a girlfriend like everyone else. Someone that I could talk to, share the little things with, be myself with, and care about just like she cares about me. I know that sounds stupid. I don't deserve it."

"Everybody deserves love, Milo."

"She's probably scared of me anyway."

"Well, Milo, I think you should give her a chance. But we can talk more about her next time. We are out of time for today. But tomorrow night is our open meeting teen depression group. Dr. Henley said that you'd be joining us. I'm excited to see you there. We meet downstairs in the conference room off the lobby. Conference room A. Room B is for alcoholics anonymous," Jessica explains.

"I'm well on my way to inclusion in that group as well."

"We can talk about the generalities of that in the group tomorrow night, okay, Milo?" Jessica bids farewell to me and points me down the hall to the door to the waiting room, where Mom waits.

"How did that go, Milo?" Mom wonders.

"Well, I'm not cured, if that's what you're wondering."

"Of course not. I know that this will take some time."

"Mom, I may never be cured. Depression can last a lifetime."

"But with medication and psychotherapy, it can be managed, and you'll be able to live a fulfilling, productive life."

"Mom, can we please not talk. I'm not in a good mood, and I'm all talked out for the time being."

"Well, I can just drop you off at school then," Mom says, turning onto Valley View Road and speeding up for the three-mile drive to the high school, where we part in silence.

Once inside, Wyatt rushes me into the boys' bathroom. We wait until the bell sounds, and everyone runs out. Wyatt checks the stalls to make sure nobody is listening.

"What's up? We're late for class. You're going to get written up. It's the first week of classes."

"You know that chick, Violet?" Wyatt asks.

"The loud one?"

"The pretty fucking hot one. Anyway, it's not about her. She was asking for her friend, Mia, that quiet one who's homeschooled." Wyatt beams in excitement.

"Mia. Mr. Callan's daughter at our piano lessons?"

"She's into you, buddy." Wyatt hoots.

"She did not say that."

"A hundred bucks says she did," Wyatt swears.

"After my scene in her dad's piano studio? If true, that means she's fucking nuts."

"So, I should tell Violet that you're not interested?" Wyatt starts to walk away, but I rush to block the door.

"No. That's not what I said."

"Milo, I think she fell for you before you fell flat on your face, buddy."

"Get to class. And don't say anything to Violet until I think of something good to tell her."

After school, I stopped by the classes I missed early this morning to pick up any assignments. Upon leaving, I eye Wyatt down the hall, one arm outstretched against the wall where Violet has her back up against the metal lockers. They are in their own world and almost miss me ambling past.

"Hey, there's your friend," Violet says.

"Hey, buddy, where are you headed? Say, you know Violet here, right?" Wyatt asks.

"Yeah. Hey, Violet."

"So, Milo. Wyatt tells me that you used to be on the track team?" Violet wonders.

"Yeah, what about it?" I ask casually.

"My friend Mia and I run every day after school. Anywhere between ten and twenty miles, if we're not working out. Anyway, I asked Wyatt if you guys would like to join us today?" Violet says, being awfully forward.

"And what did Wyatt say?"

"I thought I'd leave that up to you, buddy. I can run as far and hard as anyone, so I'm up for it."

"Didn't you flunk out of gym class?" I chuckle.

"I'm here for you, buddy. If you want to run, I can run."

"Okay, Violet. I guess that we're running with you guys. Are you sure that it's okay with Mia?"

"She'll be ecstatic."

Wyatt and I change into shorts and t-shirts at his house while Violet's down the block at her house, putting a fashionable sports tank top over some yoga pants. Then we meet up to walk the rest of the way to Mia's house, where we find her flipping out on the front lawn.

"What is he doing here?" Mia yells and points at me.

"I invited both of them to run with us this afternoon," Violet says, stretching like it's no big deal.

"If you want, I can go." I begin to walk away, but Mia calms down.

"No, stay. I mean that you can stay if you want. I don't care," Mia darts off into the street, and Violet catches up with her.

Wyatt and I pull up behind them as they jog down Pioneer Trail across the highway overpass into the adjacent suburb. We run down the river on Ferry Road, then up towards one of the county parks, where we run through the wooded trail around the lake and down Bush Lake Road to the abandoned ski lifts and the path around the lake over by the community college. After two times around the lake, Wyatt overdramatizes a collapse onto the grassy area beside the small waterfalls that look out over the lake towards the glass office towers on the business campus across the highway.

"I just want to chill out here. Come back this way and pick me up. By then, I'll catch my second wind and be able to run home," Wyatt pants.

I wave him off and follow the girls who run down American Blvd toward the Mall of America, about four more miles, then turn around to head back to pick up Wyatt. Once there, Violet sits next to Wyatt while I follow Mia, who will walk once around the lake.

"You don't have to follow me," Mia says.

"I know that. I just thought that I'd keep you company. But if you don't want me, too, then—"

"No, you can—"

We stand together on the busy paved path where business people in suits walk around us to get to the bus stop. She looks into my eyes. I see such calmness in hers. I wonder what she sees in mine. Chaos?

"I'm sorry about my seizure on your dad's floor."

"Your mom said that you have epilepsy and that you're depressed," Mia reveals my mother's words, but it sounds more like a question.

"Yeah, I have both epilepsy and major depressive disorder."

"I've got depression, too, I think. But my parents don't want to deal with something wrong with me, so they threaten to put me in the psych ward if I ask to go to counseling. They say it's just teenage angst or mood swings," Mia shares.

"Well, that sucks. And I thought my parents were bad, putting me on all sorts of meds and ignoring me while I'm out in my woodshop."

"It's part of the reason why I run. Depression can't hit a moving target," Mia giggles.

She looks so beautiful, with strands of hair coming

loose from her ponytail and blowing in the wind. A random leaf falls atop her head, and I pick it off to see her smile.

"Thanks."

"No problem. You should come. Say I'm joining this depression group for teens tomorrow night. Tell your parents it's for teenage angst and such."

"Where's it at?" Mia wonders. "And what time?"

"It's at seven o'clock at the counseling center behind the pet store across from the mall."

"Can just anyone come?"

"Yes, it's open to the public."

"But does everybody else go to see a therapist at the clinic?" Mia wonders.

"Maybe. Maybe not. Even if they do, perhaps you can get help with asking your parents for treatment, meds, and talk therapy. You shouldn't suffer because your parents don't understand what's happening with you."

"I think they understand. It's just that we bury things that bother us deep down in my family and let them rot, as my mom says. That's what they did when my brother was in a coma after our car accident," Mia confides.

"Ben?"

"Yeah. He's fine now, and my parents' marriage is better. It was on the rocks during his coma, actually, before then, but that's all in the past, I guess," Mia adds, pushing windswept strands of hair back behind her ears.

"Maybe it isn't. In the past. I mean, if you're depressed about it, then it's not over."

"Yeah, I guess you're right. Please don't tell anyone. I can't believe I even shared that with you. Violet is the only one that I ever tell anything like that. I don't know what's wrong with me," Mia shares, then nibbles on her nails.

"Your secret is safe with me," I say as Wyatt approaches and slaps me on the back.

"You two done talking and ready to head back?" Violet questions as she bumps elbows with her best friend.

Mia

AFTERSHOCKS OF NIGHT

"How did you sleep?" Mom asks me, and I grumble.

"I slept great," Ben beams.

"Of course, you did," I mumble. I wish that I had never met Milo Chatham. That's all I need, another stressor in my life. That brief talk when we were alone on the path last night reverberates through my mind.

"What's that supposed to mean?" Ben asks. "You're young; therefore, you don't have any worry in the world."

"I have a huge spelling test today," Ben spurts and stares me down. "Besides, you're young, too. What do you have to bring you down?"

"Speaking of being brought down, Mom, Dad, can I go to a depression support group for teens tonight at the counseling center behind the pet store. You know the pet store by the mall," I set my spoon down, push my yogurt forward, and prepare for battle. Mom and Dad look up from what they're doing, look at each other, and then at me.

"You don't need a depression support group. You're just fine, Mia," Mom says, then returns to making pancakes for Dad and Ben.

"It's more to whine about our problems and teen angst, then we get feedback from other teens on how to best deal with schoolwork, jobs, annoying siblings."

"Well, if that's all it is. Sara, I don't see any harm in it. What do you think?" Dad nudges Mom's arm, and she turns around and looks at me.

"You better not make me regret this, Mia," Mom shakes the spatula in my direction.

"Great," I say as I take tiny bites of my yogurt.

"Can I go too? I have an annoying sibling." Ben chuckles.

I stand before my mirror, holding out different clothes in front of me to find something that fits and doesn't make me look fat. I settle on yoga pants and a tank top with a baggy sweatshirt over the top of it.

Since breakfast, the day had dragged on when I learned Mom and Dad would allow me to go to this support group where I'll see Milo again. What will it be like? Will he sit next to me? Oh, god, what if he doesn't sit next to me? What if he ignores me? Shit. I shouldn't go and put myself out there to make a fool out of myself?

I rush out of my upstairs bedroom and down to the key rack off the kitchen in the mudroom, where I grab the keys and kiss Mom and Dad in the garage, where they are rifling through storage boxes to make a donation pile for the truck that comes through the neighborhood tomorrow morning. Ben is sorting out some old board games in boxes against the far wall.

"I love you, Mom, Dad," I tell them and make a face at Ben, who does the same.

"This is just a trial. Don't make me regret it, Mia," Mom yells.

"She's fine, dear. It's just teenage grumblings about boys and girls and homework," Dad softens the blow to my mom as to what this excursion is.

It takes less than ten minutes to get to the counseling center, where I see Milo waiting outside, leaning back against the building, one leg bent and running his fingers through his thick, wavy locks.

"I didn't know if you'd show up or not, but I took a chance and waited for you," Milo holds the building door open for me.

It opens onto a lobby with a large conference room to each side and elevators down a hall straight ahead of us. Milo gestures to me to the left, and we enter a space of about twenty teenagers, some of whom floor me with their presence. Rory and Kira are both here. They are the gorgeous piano students I imagine had everything going for them. What the hell are they doing here?

"Let's sit here by the door," Milo pulls two more chairs off the stacks against the wall.

"Okay," I reply and take in the appearances of the other teens. There are some good-looking people in here. What the hell is wrong with their lives? An attractive lady with a dirty-blonde bob enters and sits at an empty chair across the room from us.

"That's my new therapist," Milo informs me. "She's pretty nice, I think. I've only seen her once after, well, you know."

"It's good to see you all. And it's especially nice to see new faces, too. My name is Jessica Walsh, and I'm the facilitator of this group, in addition to being a psychologist and family counselor here at this clinic," she says as she takes a sip of her coffee cup." You can call me Jessica. It's not necessary, especially if this is your first day, but does anyone want to introduce themselves to the group?"

"Can I go first?" Rory asks, fidgeting beside Jessica.

"Okay, last week we decided our topic this week would be the dangers of social media. You can either share something on your mind with the group or open up the topic. Go ahead, Rory," Jessica says.

"Hi, everyone. I'm Rory. I want to know why do the doctors even share our diagnosis with us? Now I feel like I have this weight on my shoulders to battle something I didn't know existed a few months ago."

A girl to our left responds, "Hi, everyone. I'm Harper. And I think knowing our diagnosis, even though it makes us crazier, helps us check all the boxes on how to cope with it or, hopefully, eventually overcome it. You know what they say: know thy enemy."

"Plus, what we resist, persists," says a short, younger guy nearest Jessica.

"Your name?" Jessica says to him.

Hi everyone. "My name is Gavin. I think putting blinders on makes the battle more difficult," Gavin adds. "We need to be aware of our depression and all its forms, sources, and successes in fighting it so we can get on with our lives."

"I'm just saying I don't think we need to worry about what it is or isn't called and just try and get through the effin day," Rory says. "I don't like how we have to battle or fight it. It's enough getting out of bed each morning without having this barrier in front of us every moment of the day. Let our parents worry about it and just let me sleep in and stop going to constant classes intended to get me out of this funk," Rory wipes his eyes.

"I understand how difficult this is for all of you. This is relatively new for some of you, and for others, this has been an ongoing challenge for many years. I'm seeing younger cases all the time. Trying to heal the littlest minds is nerve-wracking for us therapists. I know it must be excruciating for those suffering with it," Jessica tells the group.

"At least you guys have family and friends helping you deal with the depression and its symptoms. I don't have anybody. Who do you call when you're stuck in this maze of melancholy? I graduate this year. What happens to me then? If I don't have support as a kid, what the hell happens to me when I turn eighteen?"

"Your name, please?" Jessica points with an outstretched arm.

"Oh, hi everyone, I'm Aidan."

"Aidan, you can call me and chat if you want?" Rory offers.

"Thanks, Rory."

"I'll get you my number after group," Rory adds.

"Does anybody care to address our topic this week?" Jessica asks.

"You mean FOMO?" Harper asks.

"Tell the group what that means for anybody that may not know," Jessica suggests.

"Fear of missing out. Sorry. I'm agitated and have a piercing headache. FOMO means that you're constantly checking your socials to see the updates of everybody you know to compare yourself to their busy lifestyles when we know a lot of it is bullshit."

"Language, Harper," Jessica snaps.

"I'm just saying that not everybody has this mind-blowing social calendar we think they do. I mean, have you ever seen someone so attractive that you think that every minute of their life must be ice cream and giggles?" Harper finishes.

I look over at Rory and Kira and remember how I thought that he must be a popular football player and her a soccer star or cheerleader. It turns out they're average like me. Kira catches me staring at her. I turn away and focus on Jessica.

"So, what is the solution to FOMO?" "Cut back on screen time," Rory responds.

"I know it's difficult considering how addictive it is, but what are some ways to handle this problem that don't make the depression deeper and more painful?" Jessica asks.

"Deleting some socials and keeping like only one and don't check it constantly," Aidan says. "I don't have that problem because I don't have any friends."

I think of how fortunate I am to have Violet. I'll never take her for granted again. I readjust myself in my chair, cross one foot over the other leg, and allow one leg to dangle, accidentally bumping into Milo's leg. Immediately, I pull back, but he turns and smiles that incredible grin and whispers that it's okay. So, I focus on Jessica and let the leg drop against him again, and heat surges from my head to my toes. It's electric. Incredible. I've never felt this way before. Talk about mind-blowing. I look up, and a different girl is talking.

"Identity crisis added to the depression makes for deep loneliness, as Aidan spoke of before. I mean. I don't know if I'm gay or bi or what. I'm sorry, but I feel those with plain depression have it easy, and I'm sorry to say, but you should stop whining." The girl covers her face with her hands and begins crying.

"Thank you for being brutally honest about your feelings, Brielle. But no depression is better or worse than the other. It's all despair and suffering, and we need to work towards diminishing it with medication management and psychotherapy," Jessica says.

"And this group," Rory adds.

"This brings up the subject of co-occurring disorders. Many times, depression has this ugly partner that is always tugging the little successes downward or doubling down on the pain and suffering. Would any of you like to talk about a co-occurring disorder?" Jessica asks.

"You mean like my bipolar disorder?" Kira raises her hand and asks. "Hi everyone, I'm Kira."

"Yes, Kira," Jessica responds.

"Or like alcoholism and depression?" Aidan wonders.

"Self-harm and depression here," Gavin raises his hand, and his sweatshirt falls slightly to show the cutting scars on his wrist. After other strangers speak for a good half hour about socials, Jessica takes control of room.

"Why don't we each write up something short to contribute next week, and we'll go around the room and read it to the group. It can be about anything from your diagnosis, anything bothering you, or a poem; it doesn't matter. I'd just like to hear each and every one of you talk and share something next week. How does that sound?"

Everyone in the room claps their hands and stands to begin clearing the floor and stacking the chairs to their original spots against the wall.

"Would you like me to introduce you to Jessica?" Milo asks.

"Sure," I reply.

We stand in line behind Rory and Kira, who are speaking with Jessica about their therapy appointments. Jessica shares about her vacation for an extended weekend beginning tomorrow. Then they turn and see me.

"Hi, Mia," Kira smiles, and she looks gorgeous.

"Jessica, this is my friend, Mia," Milo introduces.

"Well, hello, Mia, and I hope you feel welcome to our group. We're fortunate to have you here."

"Yeah, thank you. It almost wasn't the case. My parents don't want me to get counseling for depression when it's probably just teen angst," I spill and realize it may have been too much right away.

"Mr. and Mrs. Callan don't believe in psychotherapy? How do you cope without meds? Oh, damn, you need to get in to see someone, right, Jessica?" Rory says while Kira hugs me.

"If you'd like, Mia. I can talk to your parents for you and see if we can get you in to see the doctor who would then refer you to one of our psychologists or counselors, maybe even me," Jessica empathizes. "Nobody should have to suffer when help is available." "I'm worried my parents will feel like I'm ambushing them. Maybe I'll try talking to them again first."

"Okay. But just know that I'm here for you. Let me get you my business card," Jessica says as she turns to fumble through her purse.

Meanwhile, Kira, who's my height, even though she's two years younger than me, hugs me again. She whispers, "Any time you want to talk or get a mocha frappé, I'm here for you. Hey, let's connect on socials." Kira takes out her phone and gestures to my hand, which holds mine tightly.

After a few more minutes of meaningless conversation about social media, Milo and I part ways with Jessica and the twins. Milo texts his mom that he's got a ride home and joins me at the historic coffee shop near the light rail line, which is still under construction and used as a running circuit interconnecting the suburbs. We watch some runners on the street-lamp-lighted gravel-covered path, then go inside one of the private study rooms to have our coffee.

Our legs touch underneath when we sit at the small, wobbly Ikea-type wooden table and chair set. I apologize, but again he tells me there's no need. Every time I touch this guy, the connection is electric. We sit and stare into each other's eyes, occasionally giggling and taking in a gorgeous smile.

"Don't' do that," I say.

"Do what?" Milo asks.

"Look at me the way you do," I admit. "I'm embarrassed by your attention."

"Why?" he wonders.

"I don't think I deserve it. I mean, look at me," I confess and point at myself from face to feet.

"I am looking at you, and I see someone beautiful and smart and sweet."

"Look at you, Milo; you're handsome, athletic, and nice. You should be having coffee with someone like Kira or Violet. They're attractive."

"They may be, but Mia, you're stunning. I've thought so since the first time I saw you and left that wonderful impression upon you and your family," Milo chuckles. "I mean. What the hell did you think of me?"

"I felt so bad for you. It looked like you lost a good deal of blood from that head wound." I set my coffee cup down and wrap my hands around it.

"That's not all I lost," Milo's face flushes.

"I know my dad said you lost control of your bladder, but I couldn't see it from where I was standing, if that's what you mean."

I wind loose hair around my ears and then put my hands back around my coffee cup. In doing so, I put my hands within reach of Milo's, and he inches his up to mine and taps my hands with his fingers. I take a deep breath, and he asks if I'm okay. I nod, and he takes one hand in his and squeezes gently.

"I haven't been interested in something in so long; I forgot how excitement felt. But I'm interested in getting to know you better, Mia."

"I think that I'd like that. And I think that I know what you mean. My mind is teeming with excitement."

"Would you and Violet be okay with me running with you two for a few days, like through the weekend? Then if it isn't working out, I can back off," Milo asks timidly.

"Sure, what about Wyatt?"

"Wyatt is in pain from the running we did last night. He's too proud to admit it, but he's at home in front of the TV with ice on his calves and ankles," Milo chortles.

"Oh, my, god. Are you serious?" I giggle while covering my mouth. I wish my teeth were whiter. I need to use one of those teeth-whitening kits.

"Don't cover your face when you laugh. You have a beautiful smile. Please don't be shy about showing it. Okay?" He has the deepest, warmest brown eyes and a full head of chin-length wavy locks.

After we finish our cold coffee, we leave through the French doors out onto the patio to the side of the quaint, hundred-year-old, red brick farmhouse turned café. It's dark outside, and when we bump arms, he takes the opportunity to put my hand in his as we walk out to my parents' SUV.

Once in the vehicle, we make eye contact again and giggle. After I drop him off at his family's contemporary two-story with metal and stone accents and floor-to-ceiling windows revealing a well-lit, sparsely-furnished living room of modern pieces in white and varied shades of grey, he whispers that he likes me. I can't stop smiling. My mind is swirling in such a way that I can't find the words until he's walking up the stone pavers to his all-glass front door where a woman peers at me under the dome light.

"I like you, too," I whisper as I watch him then back out and speed down the street screaming. "I think that I might have a boyfriend."

Milo

ALL GLITTERING ABOUT
THE GRAVE

"She's a lovely young lady, Milo. How did the support group go tonight? A little long?" my mother, Traci, asks, looking out to the driveway while I slip my shoes under the cubbies in the mudroom.

"We went out for coffee afterward," I reply

"Milo, you're having trouble sleeping as it is," my dad, Terry, interjects.

"Plus, we don't know what caffeine does for your seizures, sweetie."

"Please, let me be a teenager meeting a new girl for a freakin' cup of coffee instead of a disabled dork that pees all over her floor."

"I should never have taught him that word," Terry says.

"Honey, everyone knows what a dork is. You don't have to be born in the eighties," Traci adds.

"Try lame-o, Dad," Beckett adds.

I shake my head and go up to my bedroom and flip the blinds and blackout curtains switch. The room is cleaner than I left it. Either Mom or Esther, the cleaning lady, has been in here. Esther is friendly, so I don't know which one I'm more embarrassed to see my crap all over the place. My little piles of dirty clothes have been cleaned and are now folded on the nicely made bed, empty food containers removed, my books stacked neatly, and my sketchbooks appropriately aligned on the drafting table, plus everything's dusted. It definitely was Esther. Mom hates to dust.

I plop down on the bed, roll over, and open up my laptop to enjoy a larger pic of Mia from her socials. Damn, she's beautiful: olive skin, deep mahogany tresses, warm, thoughtful eyes, perfect nose, and slightly plump lips. Exotic. If anything could be wrong with her, it's that she's a little thin, but it must just be all those miles she racks up each week. Miles which I'll accompany her tomorrow. I better get in the shower and get some sleep.

Three hours later, I bolt upright from my spot on the bed nearest the door. I swear I heard breaking glass like I do many a night. Upon using the toilet, I stand and see my reflection, only to be confronted with the fact that I'm a gangly dingus who probably looks like a buffoon running alongside Mia and Violet. I ball up the hand towel and throw it at the mirror. It isn't rewarding enough, so I kick the wastebasket and yell. I'm a fucking idiot.

"Honey, nightmares again? Don't cry. It will be okay?" Traci gets a cool washcloth to wipe down my sweaty forehead.

"Is he okay?" Terry asks while putting on his robe

atop his pajamas. "Just nightmares again?"

Yeah, that's all, Dad. Your son wakes up drenched in sweat, yelling, and causing a commotion in the bathroom in the middle of the night but chalk it off to bad dreams. Just go on with your life. I don't deserve your attention in the first fucking place. I'm just your ugly offspring, too hideous for a cosmetic surgeon father. Someone perfectly sculpted like Rory should be your son. Mom rushes to get my meds.

"Here you go, sweetie," Traci hands me a water bottle and begins the pill-popping parade. "How do you feel, honey? Any better?"

"Mom, it's like I'm on this edge of madness. I feel so sad but wired. It's like I just want to run out into the street and scream."

Do I hold back? Or share with her the thoughts of death and suicide? What's fucking normal?

"You're just overtired, sweetie. Plus, you had that coffee before you went to bed. We need to make a mental note not to do that again. You're a good boy. We just have to get the seizures under control, then work on this depression, and you'll be taking things in stride and showing the world your talents," Traci continues to wipe down my forehead. "And now you've got a pretty girlfriend to do things with each day."

"Just another day and night in the life of a nobody. Mia's probably talking to her friend about me. I'm a laughing stock, Mom," I say, wiping tears from my eyes and kicking the waste can across the tiled floor. "Yeah, she probably just felt sorry for me and asked me out for coffee," I say, then laugh freakishly.

Dad rushes to the door. "What was that sound? Is he having seizures again?"

"No, we just bumped the wastebasket, honey. You can go to bed," Traci soothes me by massaging my temples. "We're fine."

"That's a fucking four-letter word: fine."

But Dad takes the opportunity to distance himself from me and return to bed. Mom helps me to the drafting table and adjusts the ambient light in the room before she goes down to get a cup of hot cocoa. When I see the screen flicker, I look to my laptop on the bed. It's an update on Mia's socials.

"She's awake," I whisper and message her.

Milo: Hello?
Mia: Hi. You're awake.
Milo: Just some bad dreams.
Mia: Me, too.
Milo: really?
Mia: Oh, yeah. Sometimes, it's even fits of rage.
Milo: are you serious?
Mia: It's humorous
Milo: why is that?
Mia: because I don't know what I'm angry about.
Mia: I've got issues. Steer clear.
Milo: Not a chance. We're in this together.
Mia: I like the sound of that.
Milo: Ok. Great! Shall we do a relationship status update?
Milo: Just kidding. I didn't mean to jump the gun.
Mia: I think I'd like that.
Milo: Okay. Here goes.
Mia: Me, too.
Milo: Can I ask you a question?
Mia: Shoot.
Milo: Does depression run in your family?

Mia: Nope. Just me. I feel like the ugly duckling.
Milo: That's great.
Mia: What?
Milo: I mean we're in the same boat.
Mia: How's that?
Milo: It's just me. No family history.
Milo: I wouldn't be surprised if they ostracize me.
Mia: I'm sure your family loves you.
Milo: I know. It's not because of a lack of nurture.
Mia: Same here. Parents aren't at fault.
Milo: However, they do hold you back from therapy.
Mia: True, but I think it's because they're scared
Milo: Of what?
Mia: All the crap I'd bring up in counseling.
Milo: Such as?
Mia: Their affairs that they never dealt with.
Milo: My dad had one of those. We don't speak of it.
Mia: They think because we don't talk about it that it's forgotten.
Milo: Maybe there is some nurture affecting us?
Mia: They try hard, though.
Milo: Same here
Mia: We're just messed up.
Milo: But now we have each other?
Mia: Nice to know. I often feel so alone.
Milo: Ditto
Mia: For me, it goes back to Ben's coma.
Milo: When was that?
Mia: After the car accident.
Milo: when?
Mia: A few years ago
Milo: How long?

Mia: He was under for four months. It was scary.
Milo: Understandable.
Mia: Hey, this talk about it is making me feel shitty.
Milo: Change the subject?
Mia: No. I'm going to try and sleep. 'Nite, Milo.
Milo: Goodnight, Mia.

Friday at school is uneventful, for me at least. It's homecoming weekend for everyone else. I'm not enthused. It just ends in a bunch of drama with everyone getting sloshed and gossiping about each other all next week. The highlight of my day comes after classes when I run with Mia. Violet has backed out for some arbitrary reason. Mia thinks it's to give us time to talk. Or Violet didn't want to be a third wheel. It reminds me that I need to get Wyatt to join us on our run again tomorrow and Sunday, so Violet doesn't feel she is superfluous.

"Mr. Chatham, a word?" Mr. Gillespie stops me in the hall after school.

"Yes, sir."

"That was a rather poor performance on your test today," Mr. Gillespie mentions with an air of authority and disappointment.

"I'm sorry, sir. I haven't been sleeping. I'll try better next time," I promise, hoping it's enough to get him off my back and not alert my parents.

"Well, just consider yourself spoken to, okay?"

I nod, and he heads down the hall to gorgeous and young Ms. Sable's ceramic studio, where he spends as much free time as she does. In fact, they even share lunch. They could at least try and hide it like ordinary people. Perhaps he should focus more on Mrs. Gillespie and less on me.

I continue down to the locker room to change into my running clothes. Mia should be meeting me inside the larger gymnasium beneath the walking track that encircles all of the second floor. She wanted to do a warm-up while she waited for me to finish classes for the day.

She looks incredible with her long dark hair cascading down her back. I stop and watch as she gathers it into a ponytail and binds it up atop her head. She puts her hands up against the wall to lean into it and presses the heel of her feet down to stretch. Oh, shit, people are staring at me, staring at Mia. I'm such an ass. Creeping. Lurking. They must think that I'm some sort of peeping Tom. I step forward only to stumble on my loose shoelace and fall forward and hit the floor. Everyone laughs. What the hell am I doing? I'm making a fool out of myself for a girl. But, damn, she's one hot specimen. What am I saying? I'm such a freak. I shake the thoughts out of my head and approach her. She winces.

"I'm sorry. Did I frighten you?" I ask.

"Oh, that's okay. I frighten easily sometimes," Mia says. "Are you ready?"

"Yeah, can we run by my house so I can toss my backpack on the front lawn?"

"You bet."

We run the two miles to my house, then wind around the airport to the north-south highway leading to the interstate that intersects our suburb and stay on the frontage road until we hit the adjacent suburb just north of us. We sprint down tree-lined avenues of the corporate business office campuses. We reach Shady Oak beach and playground. There are walkers, runners, fishermen and women, and people leaning against the birch trees reading what can only be a romance novels by the looks of the front covers, which I'm accustomed to seeing laying across my mom's desk at home. She pauses, then darts down the hill to the beach and sprints beyond to the running path, whose east-west portions are joined by a pedestrian bridge leading to a fishing pier jutting out to the south side of the interconnected lakes.

We lean against the pier railing and watch a little kid come and cast the best he can with those little arms. Then we walk under the train trestle to the sidewalk that leads to the graveyard's shiny black wrought iron gates atop the steps where photographers shoot senior pictures during the Fall. We enter the cemetery and read epitaphs and dates aloud, always taking particular notice of where the young ones are buried.

"Do you think many of them commit suicide or is that more of a thing for our generation?" Mia asks.

"I'm sure suicide has always been prevalent, but it's the problems that change with the times."

"Social media?" Mia is inquisitive.

"Yeah, we get bullied for all the world to see and comment. Hey, look at the sunlight catch the glitter in the wind from the bouquet. It's atop the tombstone of this young girl. She was only thirteen."

"She just died last year." Mia is entranced. "I hope someone misses her."

"Well, she got flowers from a recent visit, so I'd say yes, that she was loved when someone lost her."

"It was just her birthday last week. Maybe that's what the flowers are for, so I hope they visit her at other times, as well," Mia says.

"Do you think about it? Suicide?"

"Suicide? Sometimes. Death? Often," Mia says

matter of factly.

"I know what you mean," I say, relating to the morbid thoughts. "Is it nothingness? Will the pain be gone for good?"

"Will we feel equal finally?" Mia adds.

"Equal?" I'm curious if she feels the same way I do.

"I don't' feel I measure up to all the other girls. They're all so skinny and curvy at the same time. I mean, Violet is so vivacious. Kira is so beautiful. And then there's me. I'm a chubby tomboy."

I stop on a dime and swing around to look at her. "Violet, you're rail thin and so exotic with your olive skin and dark hair and warm eyes." I shake my head. "No, you can't put yourself down like that. I mean that I understand the depression but not the body image insecurities for someone like you."

"Someone like me?" Mia says sheepishly.

"You're hot," I confess. "I'm glad that you don't go to my school because you'd surely be dating someone already. And you'd never have noticed me. Shit. I'm the ugly duckling here. I don't have any real muscles. I don't work out outside of gym class. I got this fucking mop flopping all over up here," I say, pointing to my wild hair.

"I'm glad I met you, Milo," Mia says, wiping tears from her eyes. "Nobody has understood me as you do before now. Yes, I've thought about killing myself to end the agony. To be honest, I go on for my brother Ben and Violet. If I had known they'd be okay without me, like they had supportive friends, I probably would've taken my life already. Don't tell anyone what I'm sharing with you, Milo." She squeezes my arm gently and then walks past down the hill.

Oh, my god. I love this girl. She feels like I do. And

I think that she likes me as much as I like her. I don't know why but I'll take it.

The run home is uneventful besides the electricity I feel each time we stop for a break and hold hands as we watch passersby walking with strollers, bicyclists weaving in and out, or old couples out for a cute power walk. It's weird, but I can't concentrate on anything but Mia. I don't remember my current project on the table in my woodshop, nor do I recall my work-in-progress on my open sketchbook page on my drafting table. There was before Mia, and now, with her. My depression isn't gone, but there's something to live for, at least.

I run with her back to her house and wave to Ben and Mr. Callan as I jog down the boulevard to the cut across the highway toward my part of town. I feel lost the farther I get away from her. Fortunately, I'll run with her tomorrow.

What I imagine to be a long night hearing my school's homecoming game being broadcast loudly down in the kitchen so Dad can catch it in his den while he does paperwork turns out to be the opposite when Mia logs on after supper.

Milo: Would you like to see my woodshop?
Milo: I mean tomorrow after we run.
Mia: Hi, there.
Mia: I thought you'd be watching your game.
Milo: I don't care for any of those people.
Mia: I get that.
Milo: So, the woodshop?
Mia: You bet.
Milo: Where we going to run?
Mia: Down by the river then across

Milo: To the theme park or down to the casino?
Mia: The casino property is more interesting.
Milo: True.
Mia: We can work out at the fitness center.
Milo: Don't you have to be a member?
Mia: They have daily passes. $5
Mia: We can go to open skate at the ice arena
Milo: I've only been down to the farmer's market
Mia: Thank you for today, Milo.
Milo: What did I do?
Mia: You let me talk about what I wanted to talk
    about when I talked about wanting to be
    dead.
Milo: You can tell me anything
Mia: What about Kira?
Milo: What do you mean?
Mia: We're friends on socials
Milo: And?
Mia: She's pretty insistent that I attend her party
Milo: Rory mentioned something about it
Mia: I'm not a party girl, in the least.
Milo: I didn't peg you as one.
Mia: How can they want to party?
Mia: When we talk about death?
Milo: I think they have bipolar depression
Milo: At least she does.
Mia: I don't want to go but don't want to be rude
Milo: I can tell Rory we're both not interested
Mia: Cool.
Milo: If you do decide to go, then I'd go with you
Mia: That's a plan. I got to go. 'Nite
Milo: 'Nite, Mia

Running must be helping because I slept more before

waking up with night sweats. Mom started googling night terrors and said it's something I need to bring up to Jessica and my doctors. During my shower, I yank on my hair to get the feeling of pain. It's better than the nothingness of depression, where I feel lost and alone. Mom sits with me and reads her romance novel until I fall asleep again.

Mia

BEHIND THAT HOLLOW STARE

The run down to the casino and working out together with Milo, Wyatt, and Violet was enjoyable, considering the slight wind at our backs and the colors of the changing trees. However, Milo's eyes were tired from lack of sleep, and he was burnt out. I empathize because I know what it's like to constantly feel painful thoughts like they're playing in a loop in a broken record.

He held my hand during open skate time as we went in circles in the rink for a good half hour. Then we went to work out, and it was fun to have somebody around, a boyfriend, that works out beside you. I have to give him credit because I know it can be challenging to get out of bed when severely depressed. He told me that he has blackout curtains he uses to shut the world out. I'm glad that he didn't shut me out today.

On the last leg of the run, he shared that he's feeling suicidal but won't go through with it because he has me now. We made a pact not to leave each other alone in this wicked world where emotions of despair run over you like raging whitewater.

There's this story on the national news where this attractive blonde went missing in one of our western state's national parks, and her boyfriend just returned home without her, saying nothing of how or where she disappeared. Now they're looking at him as a person of interest.

I know one thing, if I go out camping and hiking with someone and they come back alone, call out the hunting dogs because they did it. If I take my own life, it will be in the solitary confines of my room or bathroom. I wouldn't want to go missing and be found by strangers.

But the people in my life wouldn't do it. I trust them, even Milo. He's got a huge heart and is compassionate to a fault. I know he'd be right there with Violet to lead the search for my disappearance. Sometimes you can tell things like that from the connection in their eyes when struck by a glance or locked in a stare. In Milo and my case, it would be a hungry, lusting stare. I'm really attracted to him, and I think that he is to me. Like right now, as he shows us around his woodshop. Every once in a while, I catch him looking me up and down like he could eat me right here.

"What's a humidor?" Violet asks Milo, who's doing a show and tell around his well-kept, well-lit with plenty of natural light woodshop. It's so modern, with tall windows kept secure outside by gooseberry, hawthorn, locust, and barberry plants with their painful thorns. I expected it to be scattered with half-finished projects and standing in a few inches of dust. But he has a dust collector and must clean up and organize after every session.

"It's a box to keep cigars," Milo responds, but Violet's already distracted by a completed armoire ready to be picked up by the client.

"The woodshop was a gift on my sixteenth birthday. My parents remodeled and added this addition to the back of the garage."

"There's a lot of expensive tools in here, right. How do you keep it safe? Someone can easily break into one of the many windows," Violet asks as she runs her fingers over the finished furniture.

"We've got sound-and-motion-activated light switches and closed-circuit TV that we can monitor from the kitchen. But our best protection is our German shepherd-husky mix, Lucy."

"What's this tool and that machine?" Violet asks, raising a lever on something.

"Don't touch. Everything is plugged in and ready to use, Violet. Let's start over here with the table saw, then jointer-planer, lathe, radial arm saw, and extension tables, band saw, router, scroll saw, disc sander, and that's a drill press." Milo says as I pull myself atop a workbench and eye the judicious overhead and wall storage, including a plethora of pegboards. At the same time, Violet opens drawers on various tool cabinets to check out clamps, burrs and bits, lathe tools, a volt-ohmmeter, finishing supplies, and a quirky plumb bob collection.

"So, your parents bought you all this when you were sixteen? Isn't it dangerous?" Violet wonders while Wyatt gets a sports drink from the mini-fridge.

"No, most of it I had to earn with sales from the products I make here. They just gave me the woodshop space, so they didn't have to see me sulking around the house," Milo says with a hollow stare. I can tell he's getting bored with the tour, so I move the incandescent articulated arm lamp aside, then jump down onto the rubberized tile squares beneath me and stroll over to the grey, solid wood tongue and groove planks that make up most of the flooring. Wyatt is either dozing off or daydreaming out the skylights between the open rafters.

"How big is this. I mean length-wise," Violet asks as if she's planning on building on to her parent's house, which they'd never go for on any given day.

"It's 26' x 30' with a six-foot overhang out the back that keeps the modern profile and allows for outside work."

"Say, where's the dust? I assumed that I'd be standing knee-deep in that shit," Violet is so eloquent.

"Well, dust collector such as this and air filtrations systems like that over there and there are integrated into all parts of the workshop wherever you see the vacuum hose," Milo points out. Wyatt is dozing.

"Are you done with your inspection, Violet? You're taking up so much of Milo's time that it put Wyatt to sleep over there," I say and get a slight smile from Milo, who seems grateful that I've ended her seemingly infinite array of questions.

"I'm not sleeping and just closing my eyes. I'm cool. Go ahead," Wyatt dismisses me as my phone vibrates.

It's Kira again. She wants me to join her at the country park for drinks with some of her friends. I send a quick no thanks and put the phone back in the pocket of my running shorts as I pass by the wastebasket against the far wall that holds an array of lumber sheets. In the garbage, I see a dozen or so beer bottles. I look up to see Milo catch my gaze.

"Is your Mom wondering where you are?" Milo asks.

"Oh, no, that was Kira again. She wants me to go to the picnic pavilion at the park and meet some of her friends," I reply.

"You already have me. You don't need any new friends, girl," Violet reminds me as we leave to walk home together.

"You were pretty into Milo's workshop," I say to Violet.

"Well, someone had to be. Wyatt was in his world, and you sat staring at the ground from where you sat on that workbench. I felt sorry for Milo, who asked us over there to show us his hobby," Violet remarks.

"Did it seem like I was disengaged?" I wonder aloud, worrying that Milo thought I didn't care. I make a mental note to talk to him about it.

After a quick shower, I plop on my bed and grab my phone.

Mia: Milo, I'm sorry if I was in a funk.
Milo: When?
Mia: When you were showing us your
        place.
Milo: I didn't get that from you.
Milo: You seemed to be paying attention.
Mia: I was, but Violet thought I was
        distracted
Milo: No, you weren't
Milo: Well, maybe when you checked your
        phone.
Mia: Sorry Kira doesn't give up.
Mia: It seems like she has friends.

Milo: Well, she wants you to be one of
      them.
Mia: I feel bad for turning her down each
      time
Milo: Like I said, I'll accompany you
Milo: Only if you want to go, that is.
Mia: We'll probably have to do it sooner
      or later
Milo: Then I'm in it with you, okay?
Mia: Milo, do you have a drinking
      problem?
Milo: No, those were my dad's
Mia: Really?
Milo: No, I lied. They're mine.
Mia: Why do you drink?
Milo: To push the emptiness down
Mia: Does it work?
Milo: No
Mia: Where do you get the alcohol?
Milo: From our basement bar and wine cellar
Mia: Don't your parents notice it missing?
Milo: I take it after they pass out after
      parties
Milo: Does it bother you, Mia?
Mia: No, just a little worried about you.
Milo: Will I see you on Tuesday at my
      lesson?
Mia: Of course. Bye, Milo.
Milo: Talk to you later

"Eat the damn food, Mia," my mom, Sara, yells at the
dinner table.

"I'm not hungry," I stand my ground.

"You've always loved lasagna," Sara steams.

"It's not vegetarian," I attempt to distract.

"That's a load of crap," Sara blurts. "If it were, you'd complain about that, too."

"I'll just have a small salad," I counter.

"I'll serve you the correct portion," she sputters. "You'll take a frickin' leaf."

"Mom, let me live my life," I demand.

"No food, no group," she says.

"How dare you?" I let it slip.

"Try me."

"Okay, give me some damn salad," I say, shoving my plate forward for her to take and load up three fucking inches high and drizzle it with dressing. That bitch! She could have used olive oil and not needed to go with the high-calorie crap.

"I hope that Chatham boy does better in his lesson on Tuesday. He scared the crap out of me last week," my dad Seth peeps in.

"Milo will be just fine," I respond to his confusion.

"Mia is running with him now," Mom clears it up.

"Oh, that's right. I'm forgetting. It must be a sign that I'm getting old," my dad chuckles.

Mom and I continue to cast glares in each other's direction. After I hurry through my meal—the aforementioned heaping and drenched salad—I rush to my bedroom and close the door to the jack-and-jill bath I share with my little brother. I then proceeded to puke up all the disgusting dinner forced upon me. After brushing my teeth and wiping down my face, I open the door to find my mother standing there.

"I warned you about doing that," Mom stammers. "I will not put up with this shit. Get your clothes put into your backpack. Don't forget underwear and pajamas."

"What the hell are you ranting about now?" "Psych ward. I warned you about the psych ward if you continued this shit," Mom shrieks.

"You're joking!"

"Not this time, girl," Mom retorts. "Get your things or risk being there without them." She goes to my bedroom door and leans against it as my dad peeks inside to see what is going on with her.

"What's happening up here with you girls?" Dad asks.

"We're taking her to the psych ward. She doesn't eat. And when she does, she pukes it up. Then there's the relentless exercising. Now with that boy. I've had enough. We're taking her to the psych ward, Seth," Mom explains.

"I'm sorry, Mom," I try to save the situation.

"No. Enough of your lies," Mom rushes to the bed to grab my phone before I can pick it up.

The emergency room is full of sicker or more damaged people than me, but my mother deems it necessary that I get committed to the psych ward today. I sulk in the corner by the security guards' desks so she will feel self-conscious about debasing me in front of them. All the seats are taken, and now my parents huddle in the corner near the restrooms. I can only imagine what the bitch has to complain about now. I wonder what Milo is doing right now. I wish I had my phone, but she turned it off and put it in her purse.

After the desk nurse inputs all my data and insurance information into the computer, I wait about an hour more before we're called back and allow my mother the opportunity to spew her slew of shitty comments about my body and eating habits. As icing on the cake, she throws in the dark circles under my eyes and the sores on my knuckles. My dad stands idly by, too scared to go up against her. What would she do to him? Cheat on him again? The only fortunate thing to come out of being admitted to the psych ward is that I won't have to see her face.

Once up there on 4 North, behind the locked doors, they take my backpack and examine me from head to toe. It's a co-ed, all-ages ward. Apparently, there are teen wards, and addiction wards in some places, but not here. I'm with all types of loonies, myself included. What the fuck? I'm taken to a room that I'll share with a forty-something that had a nervous breakdown in the condiments aisle of the local supermarket. My nurse brings in a tablet and asks me all sorts of questions about everything from demographics to nutrition to home life. Man, I'd love to lie and tell the nurse that witch abuses the hell out of me and see Mom locked up somewhere for a short time.

The nurse delves deep when we get to the details about the car accident and my minor injuries that left scars. "What brought about the accident?"

"My parents were fighting."

"About what?"

"Their affairs."

"Was anyone else hurt?"

"My brother was in a coma after a head injury."

"Is that when the eating disorder started?"

"Pretty much."

"Do you see a connection?"

"I suppose."

"Have you shared that with your parents?"

"No."

"Why not?"

"Because we bury shit deep down in our house and pretend we're fucking normal, my dad will get clients to teach piano, so he won't have to work outside the home and possibly have affairs with other schoolteachers with which he works."

"And your mom had an affair, too?"

"Yes, with a guy at corporate where she was a technical writer, and he was in executive management."

"Really?"

"Yup, and he's outstanding in bed." "You heard them say that to each other?"

"Yes, they argued pretty loud. I probably shouldn't share my parents' shit," I say and change into the bright colored scrubs without drawstrings she set beside me on the bed. She takes my clothes with her. The scrubs are an awful burnt orange just in case I make a run for it, security will know I am escaping from the psych ward.

As she walks out the door, she turns back and tells me, "If it's still affecting you, then it is your business, and you have every right to talk about their shit. Kids sense what's going on from all they hear and see. They can't expect you to live in a bubble. Don't take responsibility for stuff that isn't yours. You have enough on your own to deal with, like friends, school, expectations, and heck, just living with all those hormones at your age. I'm Amy, by the way. I'll be one of your nurses during your stay here. Mia, take it as an opportunity to relax and not as a punishment that sounds like they want you to feel. Okay?" Amy elaborates.

"Okay. Thank you, Amy."

When it's time for bed, I lay there awake and wonder what Milo must be thinking happened to me.

And Violet? I just don't disappear like this. I'm constantly texting. At least Violet will call the house, and hopefully, Dad or Ben will tell her where I'm at, and they will call me here or see me during visiting hours. If only I'd remember Milo's phone number or Violet's, for that matter. They're both logged in my phone's contacts list. Who remembers phone numbers anymore?

I see the shrink in the morning, and he puts me on antidepressants immediately after I tell him I've attended a teen depression support group. He also sets up therapy sessions with Jessica Walsh from the group and schedules a session with my parents. I won't be present at the latter.

"How's about that, Mother?" I whisper as I walk down the hall to my hospital room.

I'm not in there but twenty minutes when it's lunchtime, and I get monitored just like I did at breakfast with my yogurt, banana, and a slice of toast. It's an incredibly filling meal of a grilled cheese sandwich and tomato soup. After each meal, the nurse sits with me for an hour before I'm allowed to be alone. At no point can I use the restroom by myself. The door always has to be ajar, and one of the nurses stands outside.

I attend a young adult support group in the afternoon where everyone has a different disorder or two like me. After that group, I attend one for depression with all ages. I choose not to talk in either, and I'm allowed to remain silent on my first day after the facilitator introduces me to the others. Everybody seems nice, and I feel comfortable when the doors to the ward open wide and orderlies push a screaming, restrained Kira, whose wheelchair is followed by a police officer, onto the ward. She doesn't see me in the throng of people staring at her situation.

They take her to a room across the way; everyone whispers it is for safe confinement—psych ward jail. I don't want to end up there. It's right then and there that I decide to be a good girl. That's except for talking to my parents during visiting hours. They can take a flying fuck for bringing me in here and leaving.

"Hi, Violet, how did you find out that I'm in here," I ask when my name is called during phone time right after second group therapy.

"Ben told me during my wait for piano lessons with your dad."

"Didn't my dad tell you?"

"Nope."

"He's going along with her. That bitch." I seethe.

"Don't fume too much. Your mom loves you, Mia. She was just having a bad day or something, and you got on her nerves," Violet is trying to be understanding of the whole matter.

"Did you tell Milo?" I'm curious.

"Yes. Milo says he'll try to call you during visiting hours this evening. I told him I wanted to talk to you now," Violet says. "Ben said that the doctor told your parents that you didn't want to see them, and that's normal sometimes when the parents commit their child."

"I'm torn."

"How so?"

"I don't want to see my parents, but the shrink will need to know that I'm okay with them before he allows me to return home. But I don't want to stay here another second, though, because they make me eat all sorts of food. I'm going to gain ten pounds this week alone," I explain.

"Holy crap, what are they feeding you?" Violet wonders.

"They assign us to a nutritionist who sends us a card of the choices of food we can make, and I have to fill it out, and when it arrives, I must eat it all as they sit and watch me during and after the damn meal," I reply to resounding laughter.

"How's the rest of it there? Are the people nice?"

"Yeah, just like ordinary everyday people," I explain. "My roomie is a forty-something that had a nervous breakdown at the grocery store. And, oh, I probably shouldn't tell you this, but Kira is here. A cop brought her in, and she was tied up," I whisper as I cup the phone.

"Holy crap," Violet exclaims. "What's happening to everyone. This guy blew up in homeroom, and the principal called the cops, and he was sedated and taken away. It was all because he brought a drink into class, and both he and the teacher flipped. Shit got real for a minute."

"Don't tell anyone that I told you that. I wouldn't want rumors spread about me being in here. Keep it just between us, okay, Vi," I ask.

"Okay. Gotcha."

"My time is up. Talk tomorrow if I'm not home?"

"You bet. Love you."

"Love you, too."

At the end of the dinner meal and just before visiting hours opens up, I see my mom and dad across the commons area and on the other side of the glass from the nurses' station. Mom is yelling at the nurse that she wants to see me. I smile and get up and return my tray to the cart so they can see that I know that they are there and I'm not doing a damn thing about it. It serves them right for locking me up in here.

Milo

BEYOND WHAT YOU SEE

"What the hell, Mia? I never imagined that your parents would lock you up. I guess you just never know what's going on in someone's house," I raise my voice into my phone.

"Yeah, I know. We're a fucked up family," Mia says. "You and your parents don't give off that vibe," I lay it out there. "You all seem like you have your shit together."

"Did you miss me?" Mia asks.

"You bet I did. I texted you a few times, and there was no response, so you had me worried that I did something or said something wrong."

"When did Violet tell you?"

"She had piano lessons with your dad right after school. Ben whispered to her. She called me as soon as she left your doorstep. I was floored," I confess as I plop down on my bed and glance at my textbooks, thinking the whole while that homework doesn't do itself.

"You have your piano lesson tomorrow?"

"Yup," I reply.

"Don't let on that you're talking to me while I'm in here. Mom would be through the roof," Mia chuckles.

"Yeah, Violet told me you're refusing to see your parents."

"Seth and Sara are extraordinarily pissed," Mia laughs.

"It's good to hear you laugh. At least I know that you're not suffering there."

"Oh, you know, Kira's here," Mia whispers.

"Yes, Violet told me."

"Oh damn, she is such a gossip."

"Didn't you just gossip to me?"

"That's different," Mia retorts.

"How?"

"Violet promised me she wouldn't share that fact with anyone."

"Well, your secrets are safe with me."

"I need to go but call me again tomorrow if I don't text you first. Goodnight, Milo."

I lean my head against the wall and close my eyes, "Goodnight, Mia."

When I return to my Calculus homework, my headache worsens. I plop down on my mahogany platform bed and close my eyes. It will only be for a short while, or so I think.

"Milo, wake up. It's time for school. And don't forget that you have therapy after school. I'll pick you up after work," Traci tugs on the comforter and flips the switch to open the blackout curtains and blinds.

"Sweetie, I need to know you're up before I take off for work. Milo, get up."

"I'm up, okay. Go." I say, still groggy from the painkillers the doctor prescribed for the piercing headaches after the fall. It must've knocked me out. Ouch. My head still hurts. I sit on the bed's edge for ten minutes, but the clock reads longer.

"Milo, I'm outside," Wyatt says when I answer the phone.

"I've got a ride, buddy. Just go. Catch you later." I lay back gently and then reach the floating nightstand to retrieve the remote from the drawer. My eyes shut down in time with the closing curtains. "Ah, serenity," I say. "Just fifteen minutes, and I'll take my bike to school."

"Damn it," I yell. "Why can't everyone leave me the hell alone?" I reach for my phone and catch sight of the time. "Holy crap, it's noon." I read the caller's name. "It's mom. Shit. The school must've called her."

"Milo Chatham, why the hell aren't you in school?" Traci stammers.

"Mom, I had an incredible headache last night, so I took a couple of painkillers, and I'm still sleepy."

"Okay," Traci reluctantly gives in and says she'll call the school. "Don't take anymore. Drink some chamomile tea and rest up because this can't happen again. Plus, your psychotherapy is this afternoon. Be ready when I stop by to pick you up."

"Thanks, Mom."

I return to sleep. My last thought before I close my eyes is Mia and wondering how her day is going.

At three o'clock, my phone buzzes with a reminder about therapy. I amble out of bed and into the curved glass shower door. Since the better idea is not to go through the door, I open it, step inside onto the pebble tile floor, and turn on the multi-function rain shower head with Bluetooth technology speakers.

After about twenty minutes, I towel off and dress in my walk-in closet. Just jeans and a t-shirt with a button-down over the top, and I'm ready to go and wait downstairs for Mom to text her arrival. I feed the dog and then rush out when my phone in my back pocket vibrates. Fortunately, my mom talks to an associate on the speakerphone the entire time I'm in her car. She waves upon my exit.

Jessica doesn't take long to get me from the waiting room after I check in with the receptionist. We walk down the hallway to her office, making small talk about the beautiful weather.

"So, Milo. How has the past week been for you?" Jessica asks, hand outstretched, suggesting I take a seat.

"Positives and negatives."

"Let's take the negatives first," Jessica reaches for her tablet and starts to take notes. "Go."

"Well, the headaches have been incredible. Last night I took the painkillers and have slept all through the night and today."

"How much did you take?"

"Well, two," I admit.

"And the dosage?"

"I know. It's one, but it sure helped. I haven't slept through the night in years."

"Any seizures?"

"No."

"So, maybe that medication is working."

"Besides last night, the night terrors, as my mom calls them, have been waking me up. She wanted me to bring them up to you," I say, leaning forward to watch the large turkeys strut across the lawn to the lakeside.

"Yes, your mom left a detailed voicemail," Jessica reveals.

"I'm having difficulty concentrating, so working in my woodshop, sketching designs on the drafting table, and even homework has been impossible."

"Have you been spending a lot of time on social media?"

"No, not even that interests me. Life is just blah, except—"

"Except for what?" Jessica's curiosity is piqued.

"Mia. We ran together before her parents committed her to the psych ward."

"Really? How far did you run?"

"About fifty miles over three days this past weekend," I lean back.

"Impressive." Jessica adds, "Exercise helps the depression."

"So, my night terrors could be worse. If this is what easing the emptiness feels like, I wouldn't wish it on my worst enemy," I grumble.

"Keep it up, and you may see improvement."

"I can't. The Callans, have committed my running partner," I comb my hair back with my fingers.

"Yes, you mentioned that. Maybe good will come of it, and Mia will get the medication she needs and psychotherapy like this."

"Are you still taking piano lessons?" Jessica asks.

"Not till later this week because they had appointments they had to tend to during what would've been my weekly lesson," I say, picking up a sketch pad and purple pen and scratching out a desk design while I respond to all her inquiries, of which there are many.

"Tell me some positives about your week?"

"You mean a week in the life of a nobody?"

"Milo, you have so many things going for you. Do you realize that?"

"Let's see, excellent health insurance?"

"Do you think that's the only reason you are here?" Jessica sets down her tablet. In the background, the turkeys fight amidst spectators.

"Mental health is for rich people," I seethe.

"Do you really believe that?"

"You don't see any poor people out in that waiting room."

"The barrier isn't so much money or wealth as race that keeps obstacles in front of many."

"No, minority clients were waiting out there in the lobby. I'm sure they must be in the Mercedes', BMWs, or Porsche's out in the parking lot I saw on my way in here. So, I'm reasonably sure that wealth is the root of the issue."

"We can argue politics all day, but that doesn't help you, Milo."

"I know what you're going to say next."

"What's that?"

"Just take what is afforded me and make the best of it."

"Something to that effect."

"I'm up to my ears in dread. I don't give a damn what money or insurance my family has to cover me. I want this depression to stop weighing down conversations or moments that I may want to remember, like talks with Mia," I finish the sketch and toss the paper pad and pen to the end table. Jessica picks it up and admires it. If only I were the slightest bit appreciative. But I don't give a damn.

"I may or may not have told you this before, but you're not just another shy teenager. You've got plenty percolating up there in that mind of yours. Not many kids, let alone adults find a hobby they're great at that actually makes them good money."

"I don't like being called shy. My dad constantly reminds me that he was shy, depressed, and moody at my age. It's a funk. I'll grow out of it," I say, throwing my hands up in the air.

"Well, if Mia is your oasis, work with that during your travels through therapy. If she pulls you out of your funk temporarily, just go with it. Now I've suggested that Dr. Henley refer you to a nutritionist to show you the benefits of a ketogenic diet. It's been known to help with epilepsy, and nutrition counseling can only benefit your depression," Jessica says, then picks up her tablet to make more notes. Little kids chase the turkeys behind her down below her office. "We must focus on solutions while you're at this tipping point."

"Shit, I've hit rock bottom. You should see me at three o'clock in the morning when I'm huddled up naked and crying under the shower to get rid of the sweat while my mother changes my sheets. I'm a fricken' burden to my overachieving parents."

"Well, nobody ever said that growing up in the perfect family will shield you from pain and grief," Jessica says, tapping her window at the kids chasing the turkeys.

"What do you think that I'm grieving?"

"I don't know. Your childhood, maybe? A time when you didn't have a diagnosis? Before things changed in the blink of an eye?"

"True, but it wasn't necessarily a lightning strike, and everything went dark. The first crack in the façade was my seizures, and things began mounting up."

"And what about your parents and your little brother, Beckett?"

"My dad has always worked sixty-hour workweeks, so my mom has had two jobs: her work at the ad agency and taking care of me, which is a handful, and my brother, who is a breeze," I say, stretching out my hands on my legs and leaning forward to cup my knees.

"Are you angry with your dad for working so much?"

"Nope. I know he does it so we can afford things he didn't have as a kid."

"And your mom or your brother?"

"Are you asking if I'm mad at them for my problems? Hell no. She works her ass off for us, especially me, and Beckett tries to act like I'm normal, but I scare him when I seize in front of him. Yet, he still says he looks up to me," I say, wiping a tear from my eye.

"You're not a burden to your mom, as far as I can tell. She really loves you and is proud of you."

"She didn't ask for this deluge of disappointment as to what her life has become and despair that her kid is a laughing stock in school. It's been that way since the fifth grade when I had my first mortifying seizure in front of other kids."

"I haven't talked with your dad, but your mom is determined to find a cure for your epilepsy and thinks that will minimize your depression."

After Jessica walks me back to the waiting room, I hug my mom, who's waiting out in the hall by the elevators and talking business on the phone. She smiles at me but doesn't miss a beat of her phone call.

Once home, Mom takes her call to the desk off the kitchen.

"Do you want to play a game of chess?" Beckett asks from the landing halfway up the stairs. "Dad's in the den on a business call."

"Sure, buddy," I cave. "Bring it to my room. I'll get some iced tea." I can't really say no to that lonely-looking face. I'm familiar with emptiness, and he's one of the last people on the planet that I want to hurt the way I do.

"We missed our piano lessons today."

"Yeah, Mr. Callan had an important appointment."

"That's what Dad said. Aren't you dating his daughter?"

"No. Maybe. You perceptive little oaf."

"What's an oaf?"

"Look it up," I toss a pillow his way and tip over the glass of iced tea. The glass doesn't break, but the tea spills. The door is ajar, but Mom enters anyway and tells us to rush to get a towel from the bathroom.

"I got it, Mom," I say to no avail. She's on her knees, wiping it down. "Mom, it's okay."

"So, what was that hug about?" she asks.

"What hug?" Beckett wonders.

"I just realize how much you've given up for us," I admit.

"Oh, my beautiful boys," Traci embraces us both. "Supper will be ready in a half-hour. The meal delivery service arrived, and I just put it in the oven. So don't fill up on iced tea or juices or anything. And Milo, I really wish you'd try to eat more."

"I know, Mom," I say, returning from dropping the wet towel in the hamper. "I will try."

After supper, I played a game of Clue with Beckett in the basement family room while Mom and Dad watched a rom-com on the sofa. I sat there the whole time wondering why I can't enjoy anything. I'm just going through the motions of being fucking human: a son, a brother, somebody that gives a damn.

The entire time I repeatedly glanced at the cheese and cracker plate on the coffee table in front of my mom and dad. The recently sharpened knife appealed to me. I wonder what it would feel like to cut myself. Would I feel pain? Something?

Just then, Mom snapped me out of it by asking, "So what is that girl you met up to tonight? Mia? Studying hard, I suppose?"

For a dozen or so colossal seconds, all my deep body aches and physical soreness were gone. Thoughts of Mia filled my mind. Her face. Those legs. Her expressions. That walk.

"Milo, your mom asked you a question," Dad said.

"Oh, yeah. Calculus," I lied. It came so quickly. Covering up the pain with a lie has become so second nature that all responses now are seemingly falsehoods awaiting release. Is it pathological? Yes. It is. I offer up some guesses that will trigger Beckett into figuring out the murderer, location, and weapon. Finally. I can sulk in bed.

"I won," Beckett says while dancing. I wish I could get that excited about this game.

I can't muster the resolve to undress properly in my darkened bedroom and instead climb into bed in my day clothes. The only light emanates from my phone as I dial up to the hospital to catch Mia during the last half hour of her phone time. She wanted to save a portion of visiting hours in case her parents visited so she could talk them into requesting a release.

Mia

CEMETERY GATES

"Milo, it's so good to hear from you again. I didn't think you'd call."

"I said I would," Milo says.

"You know, trust issues," I respond.

"Mia, you don't have to worry about me. I'm here for you."

"So, my parents request that I be released tomorrow, Wednesday. That means I can attend depression group with you again on Thursday night," I say a little too eagerly. I try to hear his mood through this wall phone here at the psych ward. Am I putting myself out there too much for this guy? Will I always be so sheepish? That equates to asking if I'll ever be cured of this depression.

"Yeah, that would be good," Milo says, but does he mean it. He sounds withdrawn. I'm losing him.

"You sound tired. Do you want me to let you go?"

I offer.

"No, just keep talking to me, please."

"Was it a bad day?"

"Oh, yeah. You know. It was a Tuesday."

"Things are that bad?"

"Tell me about your good news. You're getting out tomorrow?" He redirects.

"So, my parents sent the written request to the psychiatrist who'll decide in the morning. I could be released as early as tomorrow afternoon."

"That's great. Will you get your phone back?" Milo asks.

"I'm pretty sure. My parents apologized for being part of my depression in so much as all the secrets they have buried and taught us to keep hidden inside our house."

"They brought up the affairs?" Milo wonders.

"They said that we'd talk about how that period in our past continues to affect our lives."

"They had no idea?"

"No, not until the shrink told them in their meeting this afternoon."

"Hey, if I'm released tomorrow, do you want to run with Violet and me? Wyatt can join us, too. I just need to run off some of this weight I've gained being force-fed here."

"Sure," Milo says.

"Are you sure we're okay? You sound indifferent tonight."

"We're good, Mia."

"Well, then I better go. My phone time is up. 'Nite, Milo."

"Goodnight."

After I hang up, I knock my head against the wall.

He clearly didn't want to talk to me. I shouldn't have pushed about the run or meeting up at the group. Maybe he's losing the will to live, and I'm only adding to the burden.

Sleep eluded me, primarily because of my call with Milo. I wake up agitated with physical aches and pains. My entire body is sore, and I'm not looking forward to stepping on that scale which is the first thing they do in the morning here in the psych ward for patients they deem to have eating disorders. I doze off.

"Time to wake up, Mia. It's a beautiful day."

I find no beauty in life. What will become of me? There's no possibility of me flourishing, so will I just fizzle out? Am I like a candle about to be consumed by the winds of change?

"Mia?" My nurse jostles me.

"It does look lovely," I respond, playing the game. She waits outside my bathroom and talks to me through the door, which is ajar.

I follow the prescribed routine, waiting on pins and needles for the word from the psychiatrist. Yes? Or no? After the eating disorder support group, my nurse catches me in the hall to tell me the good news. After lunch, she'll discharge me to my mom.

I almost gag at the thought of lunch, but I hold it back and play the part. I'm a few short hours away from my cell phone and the security of my bedroom. Keep my insanity at bay. Keep up the role of the good girl. Keep breathing. I watch the other patients in the psych ward. Are we the insane ones? The ones with major depressive disorder, crippling anxiety, bipolar disorder, or even schizophrenia. Or is society insane, and we are just highly sensitive to stimuli? The people here don't come across as crazy, just ordinary folks dealing with grief, pain, and loneliness the arrogant or ignorant of society shield themselves from to protect their false images. Just because we choose to acknowledge the cavernous quandaries with heightened responses, why should we be labeled insane?

Despite time dragging, the moment arrived for my release. With my backpack and cell phone in hand, I set off for the first day of the rest of my life. It takes a little longer to get home. There's an incident of road rage on the shoulder where two men fistfight between their prized SUVs as everyone else gawks like it's the highlight of their day. And I'm insane? There's disproportionately too much uncalled-for stigma in that label.

Once we finally reach home, I rush inside and up to my bedroom. I've got some computer work from my PT ethical hacking job I need to complete and an invoice for a local builder that left a half dozen texts during my hospital stay. When I'm done with that, I dress in running shorts and a sweatshirt over a sports bra and run over to Violet's, where we meet up with the guys.

When I approach them, Milo's back is to me, but his eyes light up momentarily when he sees me. He reaches out to hug me, as does Violet, which leaves Wyatt wondering what the big deal is. After all, I just saw them this past Sunday.

"What's going on? Are we going to run or not?" Wyatt asks. "I want to get this over with fast."

"You didn't have to come. I told you that," Violet replies.

"No. I didn't want to be left out," Wyatt counters.

The run takes about two hours, and we cover about

twelve miles of somewhat tricky terrain along the river road and up and down some adjacent slopes of the local city parks that sit cliffside overlooking the floodplains. We end up on Eden Prairie Road, just outside the cemetery. Milo enters first.

"You guys have this weird fascination with death. What's your problem?" Wyatt comments.

"What are you afraid of, Wyatt?" Milo responds.

"So what if babies die? Or teenagers, for that matter," Wyatt snaps.

"Don't allow him to give my eulogy," Milo quips.

"Haha, you know what I mean," Wyatt reacts. "It's just creepy here."

Milo sits down on the grass in front of the tombstone of a teenager that died recently. "I wonder what he died of?" Milo dusts the adjacent grave with his fingers. "And this guy was twenty," he points out.

"So?" Wyatt asks, too uncomfortable to sit atop the dead.

"Hey, I know him. He died of bone cancer," Violet adds. "That's understandable."

"That's not fair. Cancer is understandable, but depression isn't," Milo gets to the point.

"Depression, there's a cure for it. You know pills," Violet replies.

"Some people never get helped. Or they take their lives before someone realizes that there's anything wrong."

"Milo, please, lets' get out of here," Wyatt begs. "You know what? I'm just going to take off from here. I'll catch you guys later."

"You know what; I'm going to run home, too. Mia, it's good to have you back. I love you, girl," Violet hugs me and bids adieu.

I sit down on the grass next to Milo. He's deep in thought. But then my leg accidentally brushes up against his, and he flinches. I pull my leg back, but he cups my knee.

"No, don't. You just caught me off guard," Milo assures.

"You were pretty deep in thought," I say.

"Does it bother you being here?"

"No, Milo. It doesn't."

"I know we just met, but I missed you."

"Milo, me, too. Last night on the phone, I thought you'd grown tired of me," I admit.

He leans his head towards mine, and I'm trembling—the fingers on my other hand twitch. Our eyes meet and stare. I blink first. His fingers crawl over to mine and touch ever so slightly. I reach out to his hand, and we intertwine. We both look down at our hands and then back up into each other's eyes. I focus on his face and then close my eyes just before he kisses me. My heart beats feverishly. What just happened? The lawnmower man jolts us from our trance. Milo stands up and holds his hand out for me. When I stand, he quickly kisses me again. This time I'm sure it happened. He runs with me to my house and then all the way to his.

I run upstairs to my bedroom, shut the door, then lean back against it. I put my hand over my heart to feel the beat. There's a knock on the door that makes me shudder.

"Supper is ready," Mom shouts. "You promised me that you'd try, Mia."

"Oh, shit," I whisper.

"It's homemade chicken noodle soup," Mom adds.

"Can I just have some broth?" I plead.

"Fine," my mother groans.

"I need to jump in the shower real quick. I'm stinky from running."

"Fine but hurry up. Your soup will get cold."

"Fine," I whisper, "is a four-letter word."

Supper goes off without a hitch, but Mom asks me to read fifty pages before bed since I've missed her instruction the last few days. I think she just wants to keep me out of the bathroom for an hour. I'm just grateful for being home that I give in to her without a hassle. Just as I'm about to start reading, my phone vibrates.

Kira: Why aren't you responding to me?

Mia: I was in the hospital with you.

Kira: Really. I just got released.

Mia: Why were you in there?

Kira: I drank with my pills.

Kira: They pumped my stomach.

Mia: Why were you confined like that?

Kira: I kicked the cop that arrested me.

Mia: You got charged? Holy shit.

Kira: He pulled my hair.

Kira: Someone got it on camera.

Kira: My dad is a lawyer. He'll fight it for me.

Mia: Why were you texting me?

Mia: Did you want something?

Kira: To tell you about a party.

Mia: I don't think so.

Kira: Bring Milo. It'll be fun.

Mia: I got to go. Later.

Whoa. Arrested? That's one wild girl. Milo must be right. She just doesn't have depression; Kira is bipolar as well. She has manic moments, too. I don't want to get involved in that kind of stuff.

I rush up to my room, pull up to my computer, do a little scanning, poking, and prodding networks, then respond to business emails. One of which reminds me not to be sad and that things will get better. What the fuck? I'm so far from being sad that it's not even in the same realm. I wish that I could just be sad. I'd give anything to be sad and get over it. I shove the computer away and crawl onto my bed. The fetal position helps me soothe myself to sleep as my soul weeps, and I barricade myself from this scourge upon the earth that is the blackness and lethargy of depression. But it doesn't work. It never works. The hopelessness and loneliness ooze down the walls, across the floor, and onto my bed and envelop me where not even thoughts of Milo help.

Later in the evening, tears and sobs aside, I found myself ping sweeping and grabbing banners once again. Ethical hacking sometimes makes me feel like I'm doing good for someone. It's the only contribution I can make to society. I'm not a teacher like my dad, a creative woodworker like Milo, or a cosmetic surgeon like his father. I don't bring beauty to the world in any way, shape, or form other than security researching and publishing my code.

While knee-deep in ARP poisoning using Cain & Abel, the phone rings. When I notice that it's Kira, I tap to disregard and return to my work. But she's a persistent fool, that one. I don't know if I've ever met anyone more boorish. Who kicks a police officer and then says she'll have her dad fight the charges? Then she calls back repeatedly.

"What, Kira?" I answer.

"Are you coming to my party on Saturday night? My parents will be out of town," she pleads. I swear that I hear tears.

"Don't you have many friends who can join you and Rory?" I continue coding in the background.

"I want you there. Mia, I think that we can be good friends considering some of our issues."

"Kira, that's what you don't get. I'm trying to escape my depression, not bond with it. My diagnosis makes me crazier."

"Please, Mia. I don't have many friends after my fall from social grace with the assault on a police officer," Kira cries. "Plus, there's the stigma and all the interrelated bullshit that is high school. You're lucky that you're homeschooled."

"I've got to get back to work," I try to end the call.

"What work do you do?" Kira delves.

"I'm a white hat hacker for some local small businesses that had ransomware problems last year."

"Cool."

"Kira, I got to go. See you tomorrow night in group therapy. Goodnight," I say, then immediately tap off and toss the phone to the bed so I can finish a few hours of work.

It's a tired morning when one exists on only three hours of sleep. Then I spent most of the day getting caught up on my studies. It kills me that I won't get time to run today to kill off some calories because I need to work on my homeschool studies. Mom won't allow me to run if I'm especially behind on my math. She knows I can catch up quickly, but it gnaws at her that I'll ruin her image as a homeschool teacher if I fail in front of the other moms she meets to coordinate teachings. They have this tight-knit moms' group where they share curriculums and gossip—a lot of trash talk. You'd be surprised.

Anyway, the day drags on, but finally, after all those excruciatingly painful moments of emptiness and sorrow, it's time for me to drive over and pick up Milo, who's waiting on his front walkway. He rushes up to the SUV. Once inside, I stare at how gorgeous he is, and he leans over to kiss me. We giggle.

In the group, Milo pulls down my chair for me and is about to set it nearest the door like last week when Kira yells at us to move more towards her and Rory. Milo doesn't sense my apprehension about sitting by them, so I put on a brave face and resolved not to let her wear me down. Twenty-eight minutes into the meeting, I glance at the clock just before Milo babbles something incomprehensible, then gesticulates wildly. In a trance-like state, he appears terrified, but then he's out like a light, and his breathing becomes irregular. His muscles twitch, stiffen, and then his arms and legs give way, and he falls forward.

Jessica tells everyone to stay calm, asks someone to note the time while she rolls him onto his side. She stays beside him until he regains consciousness in about four and a half minutes, but he has a blue tinge. When he comes to, he doesn't remember a damn thing. She has me call his mom and ask if we should call an ambulance, but Milo is against it. His mother says she's on her way.

While the rest of them talk about having conversations with our past about emotional memory, I sit off to the side with Milo. He says nothing besides how tired he is and needs to get home to lay down. When Traci Chatham arrives, she helps him up, and he apologizes to the group and throws his hands up in the air. He still has no clue what just happened. I tell him goodbye, but he is in a depleted energy zone where he's tuned us all out.

The last thing that Traci Chatham hears from the group is talk of suicide and how it's the final goodbye. She seems visibly shaken and stares around the room and stops at Jessica. I hope that she doesn't take Milo from the group. My hand twitches from fear for him, but Kira picks it up and holds it, which reminds me to breathe. I squeeze her hand back and realize that maybe she's well-intentioned. After group, she tells me more about her party and how Milo should come and get his mind off his seizures—take back control and have a few beers. I nod to the possibility and allow her to hug me goodnight.

Milo

DESTINATION: DARKNESS

"Nothingness. No hope. No pain. Where am I going from here? I don't give a damn," I respond to my mom.

"What? Sweetie, what are you talking about? Of course, you care. What about that cute girl back there that looked terrified for what you're going through," Mom says.

"I'm empty. There's nothing left. I don't want there to be. I don't see tomorrow let alone a future," I say, leaning back into the seat.

"Milo, you hurt your head again when you fell. We'll ask Dad if we need to go to the emergency room again," Mom counters.

"I'm tired of it all—the hospital, the doctors, the therapist, all of it."

"You just need a good night's sleep. Maybe you should take one more of those pain pills for your head wound? Then go to bed and get some rest," Mom suggests cheerfully like I'm simply sad and tired.

She hasn't a clue what I'm feeling. Nobody does. Not even Mia. Even she has the ability to run. I've lost the will to continue, even for her.

I took the painkiller, which only knocked me out for six hours. Now the regret, self-loathing, and self-accusatory guilt about every damn thing I failed at, couldn't achieve, or wouldn't overcome. I curl up in the fetal position and wallow in the blackness that is my past, present, and future. I don't see a way out. There's no bridge, no tunnel, and no paved trail towards a lighted path of redemption, where I can start anew. I'm stuck here, and there isn't any pill that can help me. What point is there in living?

"Who the fuck is that?"

I walk over to the drafting table, ignoring my vibrating phone, lean back in the mesh office armchair, and stare at the scissors in the pen cup on the mahogany rolling office cart to the right of me. The damn phone keeps vibrating at the bottom of my bed. I reach over and pick it up.

Mia: Milo, are you okay?
Mia: Please, answer me.
Mia: I miss you.
Milo: You're better off without me, Mia.
Mia: What are you going to do?
Milo: I can't live with this emptiness.
Mia: What are you going to do?
Milo: What I should've done long ago.
Mia: No. Milo

The phone goes silent, and I pick up the relatively new

scissors, put it hard against my wrist, and pull, just as my mom barrels in the door with dad on her tail. Mom pulls my t-shirt off the bed, tears it into strips, and ties it around my wrist.

"Shall I call 911? Or can we drive him?" Dad asks.

My brother Beckett stands in the doorway, so I lean forward, hold my arm to my chest, and turn so he can't see what I did. Mom's holding me tight against her.

"Don't let him die," Beckett cries.

"Call 911," Mom weeps.

"I failed again," I whisper, looking down at the bloody t-shirt strips. Dad retrieves a blue, mesh, performance-tech exercise towel from the bathroom. Its elastic properties work well to quell blood loss. "I'm sorry, Mom."

"Sweetie, it's okay. We're going to get you help."

The room fades to black.

While my eyes are still closed, I hear footsteps around me. I'm still groggy as I open my eyes slowly to see a nurse fiddling with an IV and then returning to a chair across from my hospital bed in the small single-patient room.

"Psych ward?" I try to speak, but my mouth is dry.

"Yes, Milo. How are you feeling?"

"Like an idiot. I can't even kill myself correctly."

"Fortunately, your girlfriend called your mom and alerted her about what you were doing."

"Shit."

"Are you in pain?" she stands to my side and holds my hand.

"No, that's the problem. I don't feel a damn thing. Nothing. I'm an abyss. I wish I could feel something because I know this is difficult on my mom and brother."

"What about your dad?" she questions.

"Yeah, him, too, I guess."

"You'll be here a while until we determine if your meds are working or whether we need to try a different antidepressant," the nurse says.

"What about school?"

"Do you care about school?"

"No, I don't give a damn, I guess."

"A hospital social worker will coordinate with your school to have your studies brought up here."

"When do you move me to a double occupancy room?"

"As soon as you come off suicide watch," she says. "I'm not your nurse. She'll be in shortly," she takes notes on a tablet.

"Clearly, my current antidepressant isn't working."

"You'll see the staff psychiatrist about the meds."

"I guess I fucked up this time," I admit.

"You scared your family and girlfriend."

"She's better off without me," I stammer.

"Why is that?" she asks, continuing to take notes.

"I'm a failure. I don't give a damn about running. I only did it for my girlfriend. She deserves more than I can offer her. Her hacking doesn't interest me," I confess.

"She's like a computer hacker?"

"An ethical one. She works for local small businesses by showing them where their computer security fails and how to fix or recover from a ransomware attack."

"She sounds smart," the nurse continues her notes like I'm saying something interesting. "How old is your girlfriend?"

"Seventeen. Same as me."

"Wow. Impressive. I hear you are, too, with your woodworking. Your dad said you make some money with it, so you must be good."

"Clearly, he's biased."

"Money speaks volumes," she states.

"That's why I'm here in a private hospital room, and the less fortunate depressed individuals are sleeping under bridges. They may be better off."

"How do you figure?"

"When they slash their wrists, nobody is there to stop them from escaping this earthly emptiness."

"I understand before the suicide attempt that you had another seizure. Is that true?"

"That's what they told me. I was out of it. I'm a freak. Is that why you're looking at me the way you are?"

"Milo, you've lost your reason for living. It's like you're drowning and refuse to help yourself up. I don't see a freak," she says. "I'm looking at a handsome young man that has people that love him, is intelligent, and creative beyond words. You're special by all accounts."

"Special sucks. I'm the special kid in school. The one with the seizures."

"You're the one with the creative eye, the hands of a master woodworker, and the heart of an empathetic young man. You just love a little too hard, and it ways you down. I've seen people like you. They care too much for others and then become tired when it's time to take care of themselves. You're spent. That's what the medications are for—to help you when you think you're down for the count."

"Thank you."

"Tell me the most creative thing that you've made. I mean for a client."

"Well, it isn't so much as a product but the technique in bringing out a piece's characteristics. It's spalting. Spalting is coloring wood with fungi. It's actually pretty cool. It looks so organic and can be quite colorful," I say as I lay my head back down and close my eyes when another nurse enters the room.

"Oh, is he still sleeping?"

"No, Milo is awake. He just closed his eyes. He's been talking to me about his depression, among other things," the observation nurse reveals, giving up my hiding spot. I open my eyes and see an attractive nurse glance at me before checking my IV.

"Hello, Milo. I'm Amy. I'll be your nurse today. Do you think you could walk? I can assist you with your IV. The psychiatrist would like to see you now," Amy informs.

"Yeah, I think I can walk," I say as I sit up. "I'm a little dizzy."

"That's fine. Dana, can you bring a wheelchair from the hallway?"

"So, what have you been saying about your depression, Milo?"

"Not much."

"Milo, unfortunately, has lost motivation for living," the observation nurse, Dana, reveals.

"Isn't that a given," I hold up my bandaged left wrist.

Amy quietly helps me into a wheelchair and walks beside me with my IV tower. We approach an Asian man that's short in stature but exhibits resounding authority. Then he enters an office across from the nurses' station, and we follow him in there. Amy then quietly disappears as I sit silently while he scans my file on his monitor.

"It's been three weeks on your current antidepressant, but I'm going to gradually take you off that and put you on another one incrementally. We need to keep you here until we're certain this new medication doesn't produce the same reactions. It's known that suicidal thinking and behavior can be a side effect of antidepressants in adolescents. Do you understand, Milo?"

"Yes, sir," I nod, only to feel a shooting headache.

His computer dings, and he returns to his screen, then says, "It's being brought to my attention that you told your nurse that you'd lost motivation to go on with life. Is that true?"

"There is nothing around me, in me, for me. I don't care about anything. I'm so fucking tired of it. I can't even cry. I'm drained of feeling."

"You're emotionally blunted. The new medication will help."

"Why wasn't I put on this one in the first place?"

"Well, we can't always predict how each patient will react. We can only try again. This time, we'll monitor you because of your susceptibility to suicidal ideation," the shrink says, then taps an intercom button on his phone. When Amy arrives, he continues, "I'll speak with you again next week, Milo. I hope that you're feeling better."

"That was short and sweet," I tell Amy, who walks me around the nurses' station towards my room, where nurse Dana awaits. A food tray covered but odorous on the hospital table over my bed sits. "It smells like eggs and bacon."

"Do you like them?"

"On most days, but right now, it's just pungent and makes me feel queasy."

I climb into bed and pick up a book my mom must've dropped off. It's a book of Rumi's poetry. As I'm bored, I take the opportunity to educate nurse Dana with my knowledge of the 13th-century Persian poet.

"Are you familiar with the poet Rumi?"

"No, what are his poems about?" she asks.

"Let me read you one. It is as follows:

> "This being human is a guest house. Every morning is a new arrival. A joy, a depression, a meanness, some momentary awareness comes as an unexpected visitor... Welcome and entertain them all. Treat each guest honorably. The dark thought, the shame, the malice, meet them at the door laughing and invite them in. Be grateful for whoever comes because each has been sent as a guide from beyond."
> — Mawlana Jalal-al-Din Rumi

"Do you agree with his words?"

"Yes, I think that our emotions, even the dark ones are an opportunity to learn, to grow, and to achieve a higher self."

"Are you religious?" I wonder

"Not as much as spiritual," replies nurse Dana. "So, you think that I should interact with my depression?" I prod.

"More so than running away from it by way of suicide. I think that you have an imbalance in the brain, which stress, sleep deprivation, and nutritional deficiencies can increase your predisposition to suicidal ideation and seizures. Then when your depression worsens, it aggravates your sleeplessness, irritability, restlessness, and productivity, interfering with your relationship and making you feel unworthy or burdensome. It's a ravaging cycle, but the proper medication can help. Say, do you remember your first bout of depression?" Dana questions.

"I remember hurting everywhere: my thoughts, my feelings, and every part of my body ached, and I felt useless and a burden, so I sought out alone time, so I didn't ruin the day for my loved ones. Then there'd be happy days, but those became less and less. Then I just woke up numb one morning. Nothing interested me anymore. I hated myself, my friends, school, and everything I once enjoyed, like woodworking."

"Did others notice a change in you?" Dana takes notes a mile a minute on her tablet.

"Dad thought I was just moody and difficult, which pissed me off. But I think Mom understood the pain because of my insomnia, lack of appetite, and exhaustion, where I'd hole up in my room, not wanting to talk to my friends, let alone my family. She knew it wasn't like me and that something was happening," I toss the poetry book aside.

"Do you think it's nature because it is sure as hell isn't nurture? My parents go overboard to make a good life for my brother and me."

"It could be nature or nurture. Was there any type of abuse? Even criticism? Individual vulnerability? What about comparing yourself to other teens?"

"That's part of being a teenager, Dana," I throw my hands in the air.

"True, but with the prevalence of social media, we tend to compare ourselves to others a great deal more.

They used to call it keeping up with the Jones's. But, Milo, I think that your seizures had a key role, too. And again, that can be handled with medication. I understand that your neurologist is also monitoring new meds in that realm."

"So, wait for the correct prescription cocktail? Meanwhile, should I ghost by in school, at home, with friends? I can't concentrate or remember a god damn thing. And on top of that, everything infuriates me, and I end up with a headache."

"Limit caffeine, no alcohol, exercise, and maybe try a ketogenic diet for your seizures. Once you have them under control, maybe your overall disposition will change and give the depression the boot?"

"So that's how you think I got this way?" I grab a handful of the bedspread and squeeze it between my fingers.

"It could even be pessimistic ways of thinking such as internalizing situations, permanent thinking, or fear of your ability to control circumstances. I'm telling you the meds, the right meds, for your imbalances may be the answer."

Mia

DEAD HEART [STILL] BEATING

"What the hell did I just do?" I say to the mirror in my bathroom. "I just turned my boyfriend into his mother. He's going to hate me now."

"Who are you talking to, Mia?" Mom asks from the doorway. "It sounds like you were crying."

"I'm okay, Mom. Really. Please, just go back to bed."

"But who were you talking to, honey? This late at night or early in the morning," Mom says, standing her ground.

"I had a nightmare. It made me cry and yell out. So, I'm sorry that I woke you. Please, mom," I plead while panting and out of breath, feeling dead inside but very much alive.

"Okay, sweetie, but wake me if you need to. I'm here for you," Mom says, articulating each word for emphasis.

"Got it. Goodnight," I reply and close the door behind her.

I massage my temples in front of the mirror, barely able to look at my disgusting self, and repeat, turning my head away.

"Milo, I'm sorry."

I wash my face and towel off, then head back to bed, curl up in the fetal position, yanking the blankets up to cover myself. All day Friday, I attend my homeschool studies and then work on a security breach for a local interior designer I like. He's an awesome guy and gives a lot back to charity, so I want to ensure that I give him appropriate attention. Supper is a battle between my mom and me, but she gives in because I didn't run today. I couldn't since I'm so tired from lack of sleep. I've been looking forward to calling up to speak with Milo at the hospital during phone hours this evening. I hope, hope, hope that he takes my call.

"Milo, are you there?" I say, pacing back and forth in my bedroom.

"I'm here, Mia."

"Please don't be mad at me."

"I'm not. I'm indifferent."

"That's worse."

"It's the truth," Milo admits.

"How is it there?"

"I feel like I'm a waste of space that somebody out there needs," he says truthfully.

"Why do you say that?"

"I have perfect parents and happy home life, and I'm up here moping around when there are people with worse afflictions that could use my bed, like kids grieving the loss of a loved one, those with panic attacks, or being monumentally bullied at school. I'm a wimp and a failure. I couldn't even take my life the right way," Milo sulks.

"I was up there. I know people in the group are there for partying too much, sleeping around and feeling like shit afterward, or depressed from being new at school, cutters, and those learning the cues from depressed parents. You all deserve the spot you got up there."

"So, what are you up to?" Milo wonders. "Nothing. Trying to get some work done while avoiding Kira," I say.

"Ah, yes. Her party."

"I don't want to go," I admit.

"I won't be mad if you find somebody else."

"Is that what you want?" I'm crushed but ask anyway.

"No," Milo whispers.

"Then don't ever say that again," I spurt.

"You deserve better."

"You're incredible. All you need is a medication update."

"I'm in the psych ward."

"I was there earlier this week. It gets a bad rap, but normal people go there when they break down and tell all their friends that they went on vacation."

"True."

"Milo, your times up. Let me help you get back to your room," somebody says in Milo's background.

"Okay, I got to go, Mia. Please call me again this time tomorrow night, okay."

"Goodnight, Milo."

I barely set the phone down when it vibrates. Guess who? Why won't she leave me alone? I click on the text.

Kira: Mia, how's it going?
Mia: I'm busy working.
Kira: Tell me that you'll come to my party.
Kira: Then I'll leave you alone.
Mia: Milo, can't join me and I can't go alone.
Kira: Bring your friend, Violet.
Mia: Maybe, what time will it be?
Kira: Tomorrow night at 9 pm
Mia: I'll ask Violet.
Kira: That's all I need. Thank you.
Mia: 'Nite

I chat with Violet for twenty minutes, shower then climb into bed. It's been a mind-numbing day worrying that Milo hates me. Tomorrow night, I'll call Milo and meet up with Violet and Wyatt, who will attend Kira's party with me. Easy peasy.

Once we arrive at Kira's party, we notice a younger crowd which makes sense because Kira's two years younger. But there's also an older group of guys and a girl, Brielle, from depression support group. It's almost as if they are the hosts because they keep bringing out more beer, wine, and hard liquor for the partygoers.

I refuse the offerings of the varied types of alcohol, so they bring me a soda which I appreciate. They don't push me to do anything I don't want to throughout the night. Violet is off playing quarters while Wyatt commands the dartboard.

"Whoops," I apologize for nearly tripping over an end table with a lamp. Fortunately, one of the older guys catches me and holds on tight because I'm still dizzy. "What the hell is wrong with me?" I giggle. "Damn, those antidepressants are kicking my ass."

That's when one of the older guys, Danfield, says, "What the hell? What would a gorgeous girl like you have to be depressed about?"

I have to admit that being called gorgeous by a hot guy made me swoon momentarily, but I composed myself and asked if he could point me to the restroom. He did one better, wrapped his arm around me, and led me directly up the stairs and around the corner to the master bath's en suite. As I ascended the stairs, I last remember seeing Violet and Wyatt playing their respective games and cheering at their shots. I fumbled in the bathroom and searched for a glass or paper cup to get a drink of water from the ostentatious vanity sink. Fortunately, Danfield tapped on the door and entered with another glass of soda.

"What a guy?" I clinked glasses with him, "Cheers."

And that was the last thing I remember before waking up naked in Kira's parents' bed. At the foot of the bed was a camera on a tripod. I reach down to feel my moist crotch and notice a small amount of blood on the white sheets. Suddenly, the room starts to spin, and I rush out of bed and towards the bathroom. I trip and fall, but the older girl at the party, Brielle, enters the bedroom and helps me into the bathroom and against the toilet just in time. She leaves momentarily and returns with my clothes and assists me in dressing.

"What happened?" I ask.

"You and Danfield did it on the bed in front of the camera. Mia, you were something. And I thought someone said you had a boyfriend, but you proved them wrong. You got nasty," Brielle informs me.

"Yeah, I heard that too. It sure would be a shame if your boyfriend got a hold of that video. What's his name? Milo?" Danfield asks as he fancies himself in the mirror.

"No," I whisper.

"Oh, yes, you did," Danfield counters. "And if you want to stay out of trouble, you better keep what we did last night to yourself."

"Violet? Wyatt?" I beg to see my friends. "Where are they?"

"They couldn't find you earlier, so they assumed you left. Violet and Wyatt went home about an hour ago," Brielle shares.

"Oh, shit. What time is it? I have to get home," I whimper.

"No problem. Brielle will take you home and drop you at the end of the street. You'll sneak in so you won't get in trouble, and all's well that ends well," Danfield elaborates.

As we're walking down the stairs, someone screams from upstairs behind me. It's Kira's young friend, Sadie. She runs out of a bedroom naked only to bump into Danfield, who grabs her by the hair, yanks her back inside, and locks the door behind them.

"Oh, my god, Brielle. What's he doing to her?" I plead through tears.

"Keep to yourself. You did enough shit not to be focused on some other slut," Brielle is acrimonious. She shoves me out the front door to the car at the end of the driveway.

After Brielle drops me off down the block from my house, I make my way to the back patio door. It's locked. I crouch down beneath the shrubbery to avoid the neighbors prying eyes. He's a writer like my mom but does novels instead, and he's up writing in the middle of the night on his computer, which is in his den window on the first floor. From there, he can see across the lawn to the side of our house where our first-floor powder room is located. Right now, he's away from his computer, so I shimmy up the trellis, open the window and slip down inside it.

After the hassle of sneaking into our house, making my way upstairs, and past my parents' open bedroom door, I'm finally in my room. Suddenly, I see myself in the mirror and break down into tears. The waterworks stay silent so as not to wake the parents. I slip into the shower and let the water pour down over me from where I sit in the corner.

"Sweetie, you're not just getting in, are you?" Mom knocks on the bathroom door.

"No, I had night sweats again. The bad dreams returned as well, Mom," I lie while on pins and needles waiting to see if she buys the act.

"What time did you get in?" Mom asks.

"Just five minutes past curfew because Violet misplaced her keys. I hope that's not a problem, Mom?"

"No, I guess not. I must've fallen asleep on the couch just before you came in. Sorry, honey. I wanted to be up for you to hear about your night. Did you dance? Play games?"

I bang my head into the tiled wall. My mascara runs down my face and onto my hands. "Yeah, mom. It was fun. It would be best if you went back to bed now. I'll be out of the shower and asleep in no time."

After she leaves, I reach out to retrieve the hair shears on the vanity. I open them up and slide them down my slippery skin until I reach my crotch and hold them to the side and pull. Shit. It stings. I move a few inches lower and pull. The blood trickles down the shower and out the drain. I cover my mouth as I release a scream. What the hell is wrong with me? I fuck up everything, now literally. I gather tissue paper to blot the blood, then towel off and brush my teeth to rid myself of the taste in my mouth. Then I slip into bed, where I can't manage to get a moment's worth of sleep the remainder of the night, or should I say Sunday morning.

I pick up my cell phone at the break of dawn, which I dropped near the door when I came in last night. There are about ten texts from Violet. The first couple are pissed at me for leaving the party that I brought them to in the first place. Then a handful of more concerning texts and finally succumbing to the thought that I'd fallen asleep, and she'd text me in the morning after she gets her phone back, which is her slight punishment for being out past curfew.

I drop the phone, cover my mouth, and bawl some more at thinking about what I'd done. Shit. My head hurts. Is the pain from banging it against the tiled wall, or is this what an alcohol hangover feels like? I don't give a shit. I just want to die.

"Hello, Vi."

"Mia, what the fuck?"

"What are you bitching about now?"

"You take us to a party, then ditch us. Wyatt was pissed."

"I'm not your fucking mothers. You're old enough to take care of yourself," I admonish.

"What is your problem?" Violet asks. "I was just giving you shit. Don't get so riled up. Mia, are you okay?"

"I'm fine." I stew at the fact they were the ones that left me there alone, up in that bedroom with that—

"Fine is a four-letter word," Violet chuckles.

"I've gotta go," I lie. "And tell Wyatt to fuck off," I'm harsh. There's nothing funny about what happened last night. He made sure Violet got home safe. He could've done the same for me. After all, I'm his best friend's girlfriend.

Oh, shit. I'm his best friend's girlfriend. What is Milo going to think of me now? I wish I weren't here anymore. Everyone would be better off if I were dead.

"Sweetie, Violet is here. I told her that you're under the weather, but she really wants to see you, Mia," Mom says as she peaks in my bedroom door.

"Send her away," I request, then pull the covers over my head and continue to lay in the fetal position as I've done most of the day. "I don't want to run."

"She said to tell you that even if you didn't want to run, she'd like to talk to you," Mom persists.

"Please, Mom. I don't feel good." I sit up and slam my fists down on my knees. "Tell her to go away," I say through tears streaming down my face.

"What happened, sweetie? Last night you seemed fine. And now, you're dripping in sweat and tears. Did you two fight over the phone? What could be so bad that you don't want to see your best friend? Did something happen at that party last night? You said there were chaperones, right?" Mom asks from where she's taken a seat on the side of my bed.

Just then, Violet opens the door and stares at me in my bed. "Mia, what's happening?"

"Get the hell out. Go away. I told you that I didn't want to talk. I hate you," I yell at the top of my lungs, which brings Dad barreling into the room.

"What is happening up here?" Dad asks.

"Go away. All of you," I scream and cry as I kick and flail at Mom and Dad, who try to hold me down.

"Violet, please go downstairs and wait for us," Mom yells. "I want to talk with you shortly." Mom rushes out the door and returns with her Xanax. She opens my water bottle on the nightstand and orders me to take the pills and drink some water.

"Can someone please tell me what the hell just happened?" Dad pleads as he paces my bedroom. "Go to your room," he tells Ben, who peaks in the doorway.

"Mia, tell me the truth. Did you have alcohol last night?" Mom demands.

"No. Nothing is wrong. I just want to be alone. I beg. Can't I just be alone?"

"Go get me a wet washcloth, Seth," Mom orders Dad to my bathroom.

When he returns, she wipes down my forehead and cheeks and says, "I'm going to let you sleep, but missy, this conversation isn't over. Do you understand?"

Fortunately, they leave. I listen to them talking to Violet at the bottom of the stairs. I gather my covers, turn over and close my eyes.

"Violet, what happened last night? And you better tell me the truth. I'm warning you," Mom demands.

"Were you guys drinking? Was there a chaperone? What happened after you guys left the party? Why did you drop Mia off after curfew?" Mom interrogates Violet as I try to open my eyes, but my lids are too heavy.

"We weren't drinking. I swear," Violet cries. "There was no alcohol there, whatsoever?" Dad asks.

"Well, there was but—"

"Did Mia have any alcohol?" Mom articulates.

"No. I saw him give her soda," Violet clarifies.

"Who is him? The chaperone?" Mom is curious.

"Yes," Violet sniffles.

"And why were you dropping her off after curfew?" Dad demands to know.

"I didn't—"

"What?" Mom shrieks.

"I didn't drop her off. She left early. Everyone saw her leave earlier. They said she walked home. When we realized she left us there, we left, too," Violet admits, giving up my lie to Mom. But dizziness overtakes me, and I lack a care in the world. I think of Milo and hope he's well for a brief second, then back to blissful ignorance. I close my eyes. Open them to a spinning room, then close again as my body tension loosens and goes limp.

Milo

EXISTENTIAL BLUES

"Just living takes a toll on me," Milo tells the teen group in the psych ward. "Some days, there's no feeling in my body, and I just go through the motions to make my parents happy."

"What do you do for them?" the teen group facilitator, Resa, asks.

"Well, they remodeled the garage for me to have a woodshop. I go out there and make crap."

"Like what?"

"Humidors, end tables, nightstands, bookshelves, benches with cubbies, desks, headboards, and all kinds of shit," I reply.

"Language, Milo," Resa responds.

"When did the distancing occur?"

"Distancing?" I ask for clarification.

"You've distanced yourself from the world. What were the last things you did before you checked out emotionally?" Resa takes notes as I speak.

"I've always been a little distant, as you say. I guess I focused on my socials, hung out in internet chat rooms or message forums, and talked to other depressed people to see how they were coping. You know, going through the motions."

"Anybody else hang out in chat rooms or focus on internet forums?" Resa asks and notes that everyone raises their hands.

"Randy, what were you doing before you checked out of interpersonal interactions?"

"My mom got deployed, and my dad started having panic attacks. I couldn't watch it anymore. It was frickin' frightening. It got so bad that I began waking in the middle of the night with sweats, shakes, and palpitations myself," Randy shares.

"Did you take anything for insomnia?" Resa inquires.

"I'd get up to use the bathroom then check on my dad, who was out like a light in his recliner in the living room. He usually had a glass in his hand. He prefers gin, tequila, or rum. I tasted it, and it grew on me," Randy elaborates.

"Did it help?"

"I thought so at first, but it just brought me down more."

"Me, too. That crap takes a bite out of you. My preference was cognac. It was my dad's," Kerry interjects from across the room. "Once I was wasted, I began screwing around with multiple partners to cure the depression, but it made me feel worse every time. And while drunk, I slut-shamed the girls I slept with and bullied the guys that used to be my friends."

"I know what you mean about partying too much," Soraya adds. "I've had depression since preschool back when my parents divorced. That sucked, and drinking was the only thing that quelled the depression temporarily. And I was one of those girls that got slut-shamed. Why don't you guys get bullied about your promiscuity? After all, it does take two."

"I'm sorry there are assholes like me out there," Kerry says to Soraya.

"What about you, Jack?" Resa asks after the silence looms.

"I used to think the worst thing in the world was to have an overachieving sibling up until she died driving me to school. The car was t-boned on her side. Unfortunately, I lived, and my parents continue to walk around like zombies from missing her. So, I drink with my meds to get by until the next day. Not that I hope it will be any better, because I don't. I'm just going through the motions, as Milo said."

"Yeah, and that sucks," I say. "I'm no good to anyone anymore." The rest of the teens agree with me.

Resa asks if anyone else wants to share, but the overwhelming silence returns, and she closes the group for the day.

"Hey, Milo. How is your girlfriend doing?" Resa inquires.

"She's doing well, I think. I didn't hear from her last night, but it was Sunday. She was probably spending time with her family. Maybe I'll speak with her this evening," I say.

"Well, I hope you get the chance," Resa responds. "From what you told me about her, she seems to bring you out of your shell a bit more."

I leave Resa to tend to her notes about the group session, grab an orange juice from the dining area, and take a seat at one of the tables where I sketch a few new designs in hopes of quelling the thoughts of loneliness that pervade my every minute. I wonder why, in fact, why Mia didn't call last evening. Wyatt said that she ditched them at the party and went apeshit at Violet for calling her out. What the hell happened there? Then back to the loneliness.

"You're lucky you just have depression to deal with, Milo, is it?" Tyler helps himself to a seat across from me.

"Why is that?" I bite.

"New school, depressed parent, and confounding sexuality here," Tyler responds.

"Oh, I'm sorry."

"Don't be. We're all battling demons."

"Which parent?"

"Mom."

"Sorry."

"Dad took off with my mom's sister."

"Holy crap. How does your mom deal with it?" I ask.

"She works her ass off sixty hours a week then buys groceries for me to cook for myself. She doesn't eat much. She just chills with wine and cries herself to sleep. She covers the bills and acknowledges me occasionally, but that's about as much living as she does," Tyler elaborates.

"So, what brought you in here?"

"New school, new mistakes: I beat this kid to pieces after he told everyone that I hit on him," Tyler sighs.

"Did you hit on him?" I ask, not looking up from my sketchpad.

"Yeah. I swear he's gay. He just can't stand up to his lifelong friends. It's a bitch dealing with this shit on top of the depression," Tyler takes one of my pencils and writes "Fuck it all" on the white tabletop.

"Is your mom on any pills?" I wonder.

"Nah, just the mom juice. A bottle a night. Like clockwork."

"Your parents aren't depressed or shit? They're normal?"

"So fucking normal that I feel out of place in my own home," I admit.

"You're lucky."

"Don't say that."

"Sorry, but from where I sit, you got this chill life, and you're not taking advantage of it."

"Stop it." I glare at Tyler.

"What's your problem?"

"Don't you see, by saying that, it puts the shitload on me? You're pretty much telling me that I'm a worse failure because of my family. That I don't have a "home is a shitshow" excuse for my problems that all of you do, so it makes me worse," I stammer and slam down my pencil a little too loud, which garners the attention of one of the male nurses who makes his way over to our table.

"Calm down, asshole. You're going to get us in trouble. We're all fucked up the same amount, okay?" Tyler interlaces his fingers on top of the "Fuck it all" comments he wrote on the table just as the nurse approaches.

"Is there a problem with you boys?" the male nurse asks. Tyler shakes his head as I turn away. The nurse moves Tyler's hands to see the writing on the table. "Did you do this, Tyler?"

"It was an accident. I thought Milo shared a paper with me while we talked, and I didn't realize I had written it on the table. I'm going to clean it off now,"

Tyler goes to the sink, grabs a soapy sponge, and returns to clear the marking in front of the nurse. "How is that, sir?"

"That better not happen again, understand?"

"Yes, sir," Tyler bows his head as if remorseful. He's such an asshole. Fortunately, he ups and leaves, but Soraya takes his chair. Holy fucking shit, can't I get some time to myself in this hellhole?

"Hi, Milo? Thank you for sharing in group," Soraya says while staring at me. I look back to my sketchpad. "What are you drawing?"

"Furniture sketches," I say and breathe deeply in and out. Again. In and out.

"I hope that you don't think less of me because of the promiscuity that I shared in the group," Soraya asks.

"Nah, not at all."

"I didn't go into it willingly."

"How's that?" I wonder.

"My friend threw a party and invited these older guys that spiked my drink then took me up to her bedroom. After that, they blackmailed me into sleeping around to earn them money. When they went to jail on unrelated charges, I just sort of kept sleeping around but not for money. I didn't need it. My parents give me what I need and want, just like you, Milo," Soraya elaborates.

I wanted to say, "So that makes us the same?" but held back at the thought of her being peddled for money against her will. So, I asked, "Are you okay?"

"Well, no. I'm in here, after all. But shit, so are other people with different kinds of similar problems, and we're all in the same boat: depressed out of our minds. Right?" Soraya fidgets on the table.

"I guess that we're all different sorts of fucked up, mentally," I add.

Soraya comes across as timid, maybe even fragile. Something about her reminds me of someone, but I can't place it. She's attractive but on the thin side. Her long brown hair lays to the sides of her face. She's got full lips and big, brown eyes shielded by long, luscious eyelashes. Soraya's the kind of girl that doesn't wear nor needs makeup. That's it. It's Mia. She reminds me of Mia.

"I, too, feel that I'm no good to anyone anymore. And it really pisses me off when my parents tell me to snap out of it like I'm in control of the mood swings. Do you know what I mean?"

"Yeah, I guess," I say, then I return to thoughts about Mia. What happened at that party? It's not like her to ditch Violet. At least, I don't think it is, which is why Violet went to Mia's for answers but got sent home after a disagreement ensued. I look over at Soraya, who continues to speak, but it's inaudible. Instead, my mind hears Wyatt bitching about Mia and her taking off from the party alone.

Holy shit. Did Mia get hit on by somebody at the party? Soraya's lips are still moving. Then she stops and looks at me. I nod my head, and she continues. I think of what she said about being taken advantage of at a party. What's wrong with Mia? I need to get out of here soon. And I need to talk to Mia tonight. I shut my sketchbook, look over at Soraya, apologize, and excuse myself.

After a couple more groups, I return to my room and curl up in bed. It's the fetal position that I'm so familiar with. The day has seemingly inched by, and supper is finished and cleared. It's time for the bank of phones to open up. I rush the line.

"Mia?" I blurt as she takes my call.

"Milo?" she says through sniffles.

"What's wrong?"

"Nothing. I'm fine."

"You had a fight with Violet."

"I needed to be alone. She wouldn't let me. It pissed me off. You can understand, right?"

"Mia, what happened at that party?"

"Who told you what?" Mia sputters.

"Wyatt just said that you ditched them," I explain.

"I had to get out of there, Milo," Mia bawls.

"It's okay, Mia. Tell me what happened," I grit my teeth and pound on the wall.

"Milo, I can't. I just can't," she whispers.

"I think I know, Mia. Did someone hurt you?"

"Oh, shit. Milo. I can't talk about this with you," Mia all but confirms.

"Where were Violet and Wyatt during the party? Why weren't they with you all night?"

"Wyatt played darts, and Violet was busy in a game of quarters the last I saw them."

"Where were you?"

"I thought that I was just drinking soda, but I got so dizzy that I could barely walk. I needed the restroom. The older chaperones helped me upstairs to the master bathroom," Mia bawls again.

"Oh, shit. I'm going to kill Wyatt," I seethe.

"No, you're not. You can't tell anybody the things that I'm sharing with you—promise," Mia demands.

"I do," I say as I bang my head and make a fist.

"Milo, are you okay?" a male nurse, who suddenly appears at my side, asks.

"Yes," I respond.

"Your time is about up."

"Okay, yes, sir," I say to the retreating nurse.

"Mia, I'm going to get out of here and help you. Do you understand?" I whisper.

"Milo, I miss you. I'm sorry for what I did at that party. I never meant to—"

"Mia, it's not your fault. I'll handle this when I get out. I promise. Goodnight."

"I miss you, Milo. Goodnight."

After hanging up the phone, I walk back to my bedroom with a nurse in tow. I must appear like a zombie. The nurse asks about my phone call, and I lie. He prods, and I lie. He says something inaudible. I lie. After all, I swore to Mia. I squeeze the blankets as tight as I can: Wyatt, you goddamn asshole. I can't figure out who I'm most upset with at the moment. Is it Wyatt, Violet, or the fucking chaperone perpetrator? Obviously, it's the chaperone, but I can't believe the other two left her alone.

The nurse is still rambling on. Fortunately, my roommate enters, and the focus is on him. I attempt to pull the covers up and away from my clumsy feet. I close my eyes, but I can feel the nurse pulling the blanket up for me. He pats me on the arm.

When I wake just after midnight, my roommate is talking to himself about negative comments from his teachers that fuel feelings of worthlessness. I think he's crying. He speaks of wanting to be alone. I know the feeling well. He's withdrawing from the family, which makes me wonder about how Beckett feels. We've always been close, but lately, I've resorted to buckling behind emotional barriers meant to keep family at bay. Beckett reacted with a predisposition towards being clingy with both Mom and me. Yup, my roommate is definitely crying. What should I do? What is the right thing to do?

"Hey, buddy, are you okay?"

"Fuck you. Mind your own damn business, you shit."

"Okay, sorry," I take the opportunity to use the bathroom. When I return, he's sitting up.

"I'm sorry, man. I'm just feeling guilty for being self-absorbed. Plus, I can't sleep. I don't normally sleep this much. But there's nothing else to do here but remain drenched in thoughts that we have no ability to act on to remedy things."

"I know what you mean there. And don't worry about it. I shouldn't have been eavesdropping," I say.

"Well, it's not like you had a choice with me crying like a fucking baby."

"We always have a choice."

"No, we don't," he whispers.

"It's the ability to act on it that's out of our control, especially here."

"What is it that you want to act on?" he inquires. He's probably just trying to make conversation after his rude outburst.

"I want to kill the son-of-a-bitch that hurt my girlfriend," I blurt. There, I said it.

"What happened, man?"

"She went to a party on Saturday night, and someone slipped something in her drink. He took advantage of her while my loser best friend played darts and her best friend was off playing quarters. Shit. And I was up here feeling sorry for myself."

"No, you were up here healing yourself. There's a big difference. Listen, I'm sorry, man. How old are you, anyway?"

"I'm seventeen, and so is my girlfriend."

"Shit, you're just a young thing, both of you are. That's tough shit."

"I want to kick my best friend's ass. He called me and told me how rude it was that my girlfriend took off from the party and ditched them. And all the while, she was being mistreated and worse by some scum," I divulge through tears.

Suddenly, the overhead light flips on, and a nurse stands in our doorway. Upon clarifying that we both can't sleep, he leaves for a few minutes and returns with sleeping pills. He helps us both back under the covers and cuts the light. My last feeling is one of anger. No, it's more than that. It's rage. And it's directed at the chaperone of that party. I've got to get out of here to handle this. And to be there for Mia.

Mia

FOR A GIVEN DEFINITION
OF LOVE

"Mia, I'm not going to give up on you," Milo says on the psych ward phone. "You can bitch at me all you want, but I ain't going anywhere."

"You dumb son-of-a-bitch. Do what's good for yourself and stay away from me. I'm bad news. I'm so fucking stupid. I should never have drunk the soda the chaperones kept bringing me. How dumb am I?"

"Mia, it wasn't your fault. You're probably still in shock. Recovery probably won't be easy. Just know that it's not your fault and that I'm here for you," Milo offers support.

"I feel so ashamed and guilty. Just you telling me not to won't get me back to relatively normal again," I say.

"What were Rory and Kira doing at the party?"

"I never saw them, but Brielle was there. She helped," I start bawling, "Brielle helped them do what they did to me. In the end, they had her drive me home."

"That bitch," Milo fumes.

"Milo, what am I going to do? I don't want my parents to find out. They'd be so disappointed in me. I lied to them."

"Go to the free clinic and get the morning-after pill. There's still time. Calm down so your parents don't suspect anything. Take your mom's car."

"What if Brielle is doing this to Kira? There was another girl at the party named Sadie. Danfield, the guy that did this to me, grabbed Sadie by the hair and dragged her into a bedroom and locked the door," I say while trying to wipe the tears from my eyes and use a wet washcloth to reduce the redness.

"I wish that you'd be able to tell your parents, then call the police. Danfield and Brielle could be arrested," Milo whispers at the psych ward phone bank.

"No. Absolutely not," I blurt. "But Milo, what if they come to my house when my parents aren't at home? Brielle seemed certain I'd be seeing them again."

"I need to get out of here. Shit." Milo growls deep and low. "Be aware of your surroundings at all times. Even if Brielle tells you that they're going to hurt you or your family, don't go with them. Any worse danger you call the police right away. Do you understand me?"

"Milo, when do you think that you'll get out of there?" I wonder. "I know that I can't talk to Violet because she gossips."

"As soon as possible. They're monitoring my meds before they release me." Milo continues, "I'll be there as soon as possible." Someone in the background tells him that his phone time is up. "Goodnite." Then the line goes dead.

I've been running on the basement treadmill and started lifting weights, too. The majority of the day, I'm busy fending off overthinking, unrealistic thoughts, catastrophizing, and self-pitying. Mom wanted me to help her get groceries, but I refused and locked myself in my room. Brielle contacted me on socials, but I didn't respond and instead deleted my accounts. I lack self-care, like not showering, brushing my teeth, combing my hair, or eating. Mom knows something is up and presses back. I want to tell her, but I'm trying to avoid a total breakdown. Pushing people away and avoiding knocks at the door is my go-to response.

When Mom finally unlocks the door and pushes herself in, I collapse and bawl, "Mom, I'm scared to tell you and Dad how really dark and empty it is inside me." I wail, "I wish I were dead."

"Seth, get the car. Ben, go across the street and stay with your friend, Hunter, until we return. Tell his parents we'll be back as soon as possible," Mom orders while holding my head to her chest. She's unsuccessful in ending my trembling and terrified when I scream.

I don't remember being brought in here because I blacked out. The busy ER is full of hustle and bustle. "Mom, I shouldn't be here. I'm taking up valuable space for someone who truly needs it and wasting the nurse's time."

"Nonsense," the nurse says while she photographs the cuts on my privates. I'm naked. Dad is nowhere to be seen. It's just Mom, the nurse, and me. "Why do you want to die, Mia?" she asks as she monitors my IV.

"I don't know. I'm just messed up beyond repair, tired of fighting a losing battle and fed up with living."

After they help me dress, Dad and the doctor

return. He looks at the electronic file the nurse just filled out at the computer beside my bed while Dad pats my feet in between wiping his tears.

"I'm admitting you to the psych ward for monitoring as well as increasing the anxiety and depression medications. Don't worry, Mia. We won't give up on you," the doctor pledges.

Once back up in the psych ward, I want to find Milo, but the medication they just put into my IV knocked me out.

Milo practically faints when he sees the nurse walking me out to weigh me first thing in the morning. He stands back with his chest heaving and running his fingers through his hair while she takes me to the commons dining room to sit and wait for the breakfast carts to be delivered to the unit.

"Mia, what the hell happened? I tried calling you last night, but no answer. When were you brought in?" Milo asks as he reaches out to touch my hand on the table, but I yank it away.

"I don't know. I just had enough and wanted to end it all. Then Mom came into my room, and I don't remember getting to the hospital. She must've called the ambulance or something," Mia says stoically. "They must have me on powerful meds because I don't give a damn either way, right now."

"Did anything happen? I mean, did anyone contact you?" Milo looks around to see if anyone is eavesdropping.

"Brielle contacted me on socials, then I deleted my accounts, and after that, I don't remember until Mom came into my room," I stare past Milo to the nurses' station.

Two other patients join Milo and I at our dining

table and all four of us remain silent while we eat. Afterwards, a nurse observes me for an hour until she allows me to use the restroom, which she monitors from just outside the door. By then, it's time for my eating disorder support group, where I sit silent, wondering what it is all for anyway.

Afterward, as I enter, I pass Milo on his way out of occupational therapy. I couldn't handle a bubbly personality right about now. Thankfully, the facilitator is low-key. When my group is finished, the nurse takes us down to the small gymnasium at the end of the ward, where the others pace the room while I remain numb on the sidelines. At lunch, Milo sits by me again, and we continue our silence. He stays while the nurse monitors me at our table and answers her small talk for me because he must know how miserable I truly am at the moment.

Then it's time for our young adult support group. Milo sits beside me and keeps quiet as the other teens share self-mutilation tips. I know that's not what it's meant to be, but that is what I'm taking from the group: better ways to cut, burn, scrape, and hit ourselves.

Resa, the facilitator, switches the subject when she asks, "What are the reasons you think that others hurt you through their words?" She waits at the marker board for someone to say something, then scribbles quickly.

A lively older teen starts rattling off her reasons, "Manipulation, projection, guilt, superiority, lack of communication skills, and need for a scapegoat."

"Okay," Resa says, "Let's break those down. Who wants to pick one and elaborate? Milo, how about you since you've been quiet the last couple of times we've met?"

Milo doesn't look like he wants to share, but does so anyway. "People are used to us being depressed, and we become easy targets for criticism, making them feel superior."

"They don't want to feel guilty about something they did to you," I say, thinking of how Brielle treated me after the party when she drove me home.

"That's excellent, both of you. Thanks for sharing. Anyone else?"

"They need a scapegoat to hide something they've done by shining the light on you by inflicting pain. Assholes," answers another brooding teen who cracks his knuckles, which annoys me to no end. It's so loud and echoes off the walls of my mind.

"People can't communicate effectively, so they bring attention to our holding back, so they don't look so stupid," a tall kid who looks too old to be in the teen group says.

"Thomas, you've been quiet the last few times, too. Can you share something?" Resa questions.

"Yeah, exactly what you just did. You manipulated me into giving you an answer by pointing out my failure to share during the last sessions with the group. Don't worry; my mom's a master manipulator, too. I'm used to it."

"I apologize, but I need to get you guys to speak. I guess that I could've addressed you outright, but that would've allowed you to decline participation," Resa responds.

The lively teen adds, "And people project their negative emotions out, and you're just in the line of fire, so to say,"

"Michael?" Resa addresses.

"I'm too exhausted to think. Plus, I just don't give a damn. Shit, I wake up tired, yet I'm unable to fall asleep, and nobody around here will give me a damn sleeping pill," Michael stews.

"Michael, you're well aware of why you're not prescribed any sleeping pills. Please don't use rude language in the group. And you need to share before we can look at releasing you. I know that all of you understand the rules," Resa remarks.

"This is bullshit," Michael, who has been sitting backward on his chair during the entire session, stands and tosses it to the side.

Resa apologizes for the display and winds up our teen group meeting, then abruptly goes to the nurses' station to log our behavior and comments in our files.

Meanwhile, I tell Milo, "I'm sorry that I'm so messed up and mistreated you earlier."

"It wasn't a problem. Mia, it's understandable. Just know that I'm here for you," Milo replies.

After lunch monitoring, where Milo read a book while my nurse prompted me to small talk with her at our tiny dining table, it's time for the depression support group. Almost all of the teens from the earlier group join with a handful of adults in the more oversized group lounge.

When Milo and I enter and sit on the sofa next to the lively teen from the previous group, a melancholy man from across the room shares, "People make me feel lazy, worthless, and stupid, but I'm a very creative person. I can play the drums, guitar, and piano."

"That's their problem and not yours. Don't let them bring you down," the bubbly teen tells the man.

Thankfully, Lily and Jack, the group facilitators, enter and take charge of the room.

Jack begins, "What is depression? Not the technical term, but in your reality?"

"Acute and chronic brain fog and memory loss," a woman answers. "I can't recall anything short-term to save my life."

The cheerful teen girl raises her hand, and I sigh. What epiphany does she have to share, or so I think to myself.

She says, "Battling demons in your mind all the while smiling because you worry about others' feelings and don't want to bring them down."

Now I feel like an asshole.

The teen girl continues, "And buying clothes on eBay that I can't afford to pay for when the credit card bill comes, then hoarding and bingeing."

"Watching comedy reruns on a perpetual loop even though you know the dialogue verbatim while avoiding self-care, personal hygiene, and housework," a forty-something motherly type says.

"Leaving bills unopened to the point of disconnect all the while avoiding career opportunities because I expect failure," a handsome twenty-something shares.

"Not having the energy to socialize because it's mind-numbing and because I feel vulnerable, sensitive, and drained," the tall teen from the previous group adds.

"Good. Good," Lily closes the question. "Now, who wants to share how they're doing today? Maybe tell us about a family visit or something that you're thinking about that you want to get out of your mind to release its control over you."

The motherly type adds, "I've been thinking about how I don't know anything else besides depression. How do others get through their lives without it? I think about what it would be like, who I could've been, or what I can accomplish now if I didn't muddle with this daily."

The handsome twenty-something shares again, "I'm thinking about when I can get back to my calendar and determine which day will be the best day to kill myself. I'm tired of climbing the corporate ladder while fighting with myself, second-guessing, and self-hatred."

I'm so shocked that I don't even remember the rest of what everybody else says for the duration of the group. How can someone with a gorgeous face, incredible body, and full, thick head of wavy brown hair be depressed? He must be popular and have money based on his clothes. If I had met him on the street, I would've thought he came from privilege and didn't have a worry in the world.

Upon leaving the group, Milo and I return to our table in the dining area.

"This is weird. Before, my only thought was to get out of the group so I could call you. Now that you're here, I'm at a loss for words," Milo says.

"I feel like an ass," I say.

"Why?" he wonders, attempting to touch my hand, but I pull it away.

"Because I've been making assumptions about everybody in here while they're going through the same thing, if not worse?" I explain.

"That's natural. I do it, too," Milo comforts. "And, I know that I'm being selfish, but I'm glad that you're here and safe."

"Milo, what am I going to do? What if Brielle is right and they threaten my family?" I relay my worries. "Mia, would you reconsider telling your parents and going to the police?" He sits forward and whispers.

"Hi, Milo. Do you and your friend care if I sit down with you?" a petite, timid girl asks.

"No, go ahead," I say after Milo turns to question how I feel about it.

"Soraya, this is Mia," Milo stutters.

"Hello," she says, and I smile a big fake one right back. It's not because I dislike her; instead, it's because I don't give a damn where anyone sits at the moment, as I'm a little wound up in my shitty life.

"I didn't see you in either group this afternoon," Milo tells Soraya.

"No, I had some tests. First, there were X-rays, a CT scan, and an EEG," Soraya shares. "They're trying to figure out if my head getting slammed when I was assaulted caused traumatic brain injury or if the headaches will go away."

"I hope they figure it out and get you on the right meds," Milo says.

"Oh, there's my nurse. I need to get a painkiller. I'll talk to you both later," Soraya says, rushing away towards the nurses' station.

"She was assaulted?" I question.

"She told me her story, which is very similar to yours, which is how I guessed what happened to you. I think it would help if you talked to her about what happened to you." Milo cracks his knuckles and looks around nervously.

"She's down the hall, so she can't hear you," I say.

"It's almost the exact same thing, except the aftermath led to her being pimped because they threatened her," Milo whispers.

"I think that's what they have planned in my case as well, Milo," I mumble through tears. A nurse sees me and walks over and sits down.

"Mia, are you okay? Can you share what has you upset?"

"Nothing in particular. I'm going back to my room," I say to the nurse, then address Milo, "Please get details. Thanks. See you in a bit at suppertime."

Milo

LAUGH, KOOKABURRA, LAUGH

After groups the following day, Mia goes to take a nap in her room since her roommate was just discharged, and Mia could have some alone time, which is highly irregular in the psych ward. They keep us busy, and other patients usually flood our downtime wanting to share or commiserate.

So, I take my science fiction novel to the dining room and sit down at the usual table, only to be joined by Soraya soon after. I'm a little unnerved, but I think this is the perfect opportunity to get details for Mia.

"Could I ask you a question about your assault, if that's okay?" I broach the subject as gently as I can think.

"Sure," Soraya says. She laces her fingers on the table before her.

"How did the prostitution happen in the first place? I mean, did someone stalk you on socials afterward and then blackmail you into what you did for them?"

"Pretty much, yeah. How did you know?" Soraya questions.

"I just think it sounds so unlike the person sitting across from me now. I know I'm probably saying this wrong, and I don't mean to offend you in the least," I respond, setting my novel down on the table and giving her my full attention.

"Well, after that first night when those older guys raped me after spiking my drink, they blackmailed me, as I told you before. They did it with pictures and videos they took of me during the rape that showed me doing all sorts of things to the men, plural," Soraya scans the room for any possible eavesdroppers.

"Yes, you did. I remember now. I'm sorry," I apologize, but she disregards it and continues with her story.

"So, I did it—slept with men for money—which they kept, giving me only a small portion, which still added up to a lot more money than a teen can make in retail or a restaurant," Soraya chews her lip and her face flushes.

"Then they went to jail?" I recall. "You said that, right?"

"Exactly. But I kept doing it because I felt like shit and wanted to be treated as such. I didn't think that I deserved anything worthwhile. Then it happened again," she says. "You'd think I would've learned the first time around, but no."

"Did they know that you'd done that before?" I ask.

"No, and I never told them," she responds.

"Why not?"

"A microscopic piece of control that I imagined I had, knowing how they worked and thought I had the power to make a break for it whenever I wanted or needed to if things got rough." Soraya continues to look around us for anyone in earshot.

"When it happened the second time, how did they do it? What was their MO?" I felt like a detective interrogating her, but she didn't seem to mind.

"I went to an outdoor concert with my girlfriend, and afterward, there was a keg in the parking lot of a nearby apartment complex. You know the kind of kegger with the red cups for cheap?"

"Yeah."

"I barely had one and felt dizzy. The person serving the cups was a teenage girl, so I didn't have the slightest clue that anything terrible was going to happen. These weren't like the streetwise girls I had grown to know doing what I did. She was cute in a girl-next-door sort of way. Then I remember her telling me that if I wanted the fabulous clothes and jewelry she had, she could set it up. That's when alarms went off in my head. I looked around to see where my friend was," Soraya says.

"Did they get her, too?" I ask.

"In due time, Milo."

"Sorry, go ahead."

"Then I remember my body feeling heavy or something where I couldn't hold my head up or keep my eyes open; I was drowsy, and everything was spinning until I blacked out."

"Holy crap," I let escape.

"It was weird that I remember up until one point, then all of a sudden nothing else until I woke up naked in my bed crying hysterically, my stomach twisting in knots with puke everywhere and limited control over my body. I could barely hold my head up. It was blurry or watery when I got my phone and dialed my friend by tactile memory, but when she answered, I couldn't speak. She rushed to my place, and by then, my parents were home from their date night stay at a swanky local hotel, as they called it," Soraya derides it.

"Back to you," I prod.

"My friend rushed to my room, and I still had no coordination whatsoever. She couldn't figure out if somebody had hit me or what because all the blood vessels in my eyes burst. I looked hideous, so she tried to shower me, but I was so limp. It was weird because my heart raced, with a migraine, shaking uncontrollably, and I was so incredibly fatigued from it."

"So, it didn't happen to her as well?" I ask.

"Milo, let me tell my story."

"Sorry." I look around as well.

"That time it happened, I was confused for days and trying to piece a timeline together while washing my bloody throat or something out with non-alcoholic mouthwash repeatedly, as well as showering over and over again because of the cold sweats and because I just felt gross."

"I bet."

"A few days later, I got all these photos of men, plural, doing sexual things to me, crazy ass things. They said that if I told anyone, they'd send the images to my parents and all my friends and relatives on my socials, which they bookmarked before I deleted my accounts."

"Why was it much worse the second time around?" I inquire.

"It was the different drug they used on me. I could've been drugged with Rohypnol, GHB, ketamine, or other drugs that feel like a heavy weight is holding you down, sort of like sleep paralysis while having the flu."

"How do they work? I've never had the reason to Google it."

"They're central nervous system depressants that slow down breathing and heart rate."

"That makes sense."

"Well, Mom and Dad believed it was the flu, and my eye blood vessels burst from the projectile vomiting."

"So, back to when the group of guys gang raped me, I saw the videotape. One of them petted my hair and sang me a kids' song. You know that one about the Kookaburra. He was trying to make me laugh with him for the camera."

"Outrageous."

"I started sleeping around for them, but I saw how they trapped other girls, and I felt guilty. Then last week, I cut myself a little too deep."

"Why?"

"Ritual, you know?" Soraya scans the room and sees a nurse heading our way.

"Shit." I blurt.

Soraya spills the rest rapidly, "I was certain that I was going to die. I lay there singing that stupid Kookaburra song. When my Mom found me, I laughed then cried hysterically, and that's how I ended up here."

"What are you two talking about?" Amy the nurse asks.

"I was sharing my story with Milo, here. I think that I've shocked him," Soraya says through tears. She wipes the mascara off her face.

"Keep in mind about the date rape drug GHB: if you suspect you were drugged, you only have about twenty-four hours for it to be detected in the blood.

After that, it is totally gone & no trace," Amy teaches us, or me at least.

"Yeah, I've learned that if I wake up in a stranger's place with no short-term memory, I should call 911 from there," Soraya states, tapping her forefinger on the tabletop.

"Yes, police appreciate the evidence they find in the area that allows them to charge someone and eventually turn it over for prosecution. And always get tested for date rape drugs as soon as possible," Amy nods her head.

"I've seen so many girls who are almost sex trafficked."

"What if someone is being targeted? And it's after the fact, by that I mean too late for tests?" I query up for either to respond.

"Do you know someone, Milo?" Amy asks.

Soraya kicks me underneath the table, but I disregard her and respond with a shake of my head to Amy. Just then, a call over the intercom requests Amy to go to one of her patients' rooms.

"You should've told Amy. She could help both of you."

"What?" I act bewildered.

"It's Mia, isn't it?" Soraya prods.

"No. Definitely not," I lie without shame, but the fear intensifies that Mia might find out. I turn to look around to see if she is within listening distance, but she must still be back in her room.

"Okay. Have it your way," Soraya says. "But she needs to get help while she's in here. Out there, it's going to be more difficult with them harassing her to no end. They'll find a girl her age that will work to convince Mia that she should have sex for money."

Soraya looks up suddenly and goes wide-eyed. "Oh, shit."

I turn and see Mia hyperventilating after what she just overheard. I rush to her, but she runs to her room, and males can't be down the female patients' corridor and vice versa.

"Mia," I yell after her and garner the attention of the nursing staff.

"I'm sorry, Milo," Soraya says.

"Shit." Tears well up in my eyes.

"Maybe it's for the best?" Soraya says and taps my shoulder, then leaves toward the nurses' station, where Amy looks toward me.

Mia refuses to come out and eat in the dining room with the rest of the patients. Amy questions me, but I lie and ask Soraya to as well. Mia also refuses to speak with her parents when they come to visit her. They ask me what's going on, but I shrug my shoulders and walk away.

"Son, what's wrong?" My dad asks.

"Nothing. I don't feel like talking. It's just the new meds, I think," I lie.

"Well, your brother misses you. We all do," Mom shares. "And you've had several clients drop by for their finished pieces. I allowed them to take the ones by the garage door that had invoices stamped PAID atop them. I hope that's okay?"

"Sure, Mom. Thank you."

They don't stay to visit that long considering my lack of conversation. When they kiss and hug me, I see nurse Amy take an IV into Mia's room. I get nauseous.

Mia still refuses to eat in the dining room and is skipping groups. She didn't miss much. Stupid questions to get us thinking and sharing.

Resa facilitates the young adult group again today. She asks about stigma first.

"What is it? Examples, please? And everybody has been here before, so I expect you all to share," she says.

The vivacious teen girl with all the answers shares, "When people tell us to cheer up because they think it's in our power to do so. Like they think, we're purposefully being depressed. Suck it up, they also say."

An anxious teen by the name of Kerry, I think, says, "Don't be oversensitive. Or don't be overdramatic. That's what I get all the time. It hits hard because it sounds like they're saying I have feminine tendencies or something."

"What the hell?" Soraya pounces. "Fuck you."

"Soraya, watch your language. And do you want to share something?" Resa questions.

"Yeah, because my family has money, people tell me that others have it worse than I do. Think about the homeless, the abused children, the hungry, and the down-and-out people. Like that's supposed to make me feel better?"

"I had a teacher ask me once who ever told me life would be easy. I should pull myself up by my bootstraps, get on with tasks at hand, and stop dwelling on my problems," I share.

Resa looks at a brooding boy in the corner. At first, he pretends he doesn't see her, but eventually gives in to the silence in the room.

"You're lazy." He continues, "That's what they tell me. Just because I'm high functioning doesn't mean I'm faking my disorders or being lazy. I want to punch them in the face. And I guess that I did, which is why I'm in here."

"Thank you for sharing. All of you," Resa starts. "Everybody wears a metaphorical mask, but that doesn't allow us to share what we're feeling all the time. And when stigma shows its ugly head, we really pretend things are fine. But it's okay to sit back, breathe, and tell yourself that they don't know what's happening inside your mind. Don't fall prey to their projections, I guess, is what I'm trying to say. You're all wonderful, capable, intelligent teens. Don't let someone ruin your day because they're a jerk."

"What makes it worse is we internalize their thoughts," Soraya adds.

"Exactly," Resa says. "Try not to do that. I know that's a monumental task, but even making a meager attempt will do wonders. Thank you for coming to the group today. I hope to see you back tomorrow."

Afterward, Soraya taps me on the arm, "Can I talk to you while we have these ten minutes in between groups?"

"Yes?"

"I'm sorry about yesterday. Mia came around so quickly. At first, I thought she was someone else. But then I saw the look on her face. Milo, please forgive me?"

"It's my fault. I shouldn't have said anything. It was stupid of me, and I deserve the silent treatment this time. I'd react the same way if I were in her shoes," I respond.

"Milo. I bear a great deal of guilt for being a criminal accessory to the crime of sex trafficking. I don't want that to happen to Mia. I want to help her. And I don't want to see you struggle to help her when I can share things that made a difference for me in that similar situation," Soraya spiels.

"What do you think I can even do? She won't talk to me," I say.

"But she did talk to you. Tell her parents. They need to know so those guys don't drag Mia into a suburban prostitution ring."

"What are these guys like anyway?" I wonder.

"They're just like anybody else you'd see at the mall, for example. They don't stand out because they use girls like me to trap other girls into doing it," Soraya says.

"Were they violent?"

"No, never. It was more emotional abuse and coercion."

"How can somebody fall for that? And I don't mean to say it, but especially from the suburbs? These kids in town have everything they need. Why fall prey to such assholes?" I contemplate.

"It's easy. Girls out here see the nice things others, more affluent girls have, and want those things. Maybe they come from a broken home and have stricter budgets that don't allow for such nice things. Or maybe they are emotionally or physically abused at home? Sometimes, it feels like you're in control when you get to choose who to sleep with instead of being raped. That's where promiscuity comes into play."

"Mia's being threatened with harm to her family and friends," I cave.

"Then you definitely have to tell someone," Soraya warns.

"I can't. You saw her reaction to just telling you yesterday."

"You didn't tell me, Milo. Don't put that on your shoulders."

"Soraya, no."

"What happens if something happens to a member of Mia's family or a friend? Do you really want that on your shoulder's, too?" Soraya makes sense.

"After the group, I can go with you to the nurses' station, and we'll get Amy. She's approachable and knows a little bit about what we're talking about now, anyway," Soraya plans.

"I'll see how I think after the group. I'm not saying it's a certainty."

Soraya sits next to me in the depression group, where people of all ages and genders join us. My mind fades in and out of the topic at hand: helping someone who is experiencing depression. I watch the facilitator, Lily, write answers from the group on the board:

Sit with them.

Offer to do chores or errands.

Hold their hands.

Give them a hug.

Prepare them a meal.

Go for a walk with them in nature.

Listen to music or watch a TV show with them.

Just be there for them and with them.

It's difficult having to sit through a group and do time when I could be focusing on how to help Mia. Should I tell? Maybe I'll talk to her parents tonight if they try to visit Mia again. I can get a feel for what they're thinking.

Milo

IT STARTS WITH GOODBYE

When Mia turns away from her parents again, I stop them in the hall and greet them. They look downtrodden. So, I ask how things are going at home.

"We had a break-in. The burglars focused on the expensive computing equipment in Mia's bedroom," Mia's mother, Sara Callan, informs, while obviously devastated.

"Were you at home?"

"No, we'd gone to the grocery store after Seth finished with his piano students after 8:00 pm. Thank goodness we weren't home."

"How's Ben doing?" I inquire.

"He's pretty shaken. We let him sleep in a sleeping bag on our bedroom floor last night," Mia's dad, Seth, reveals.

"None of the neighbors saw anything?" I ask.

"Nothing out of the ordinary," Seth seethes.

Just then, Mia comes out from behind her parents and sees me talking to them. She fumes. "Go to hell, Milo. I'm done with you, you asshole," Mia yells and alerts the ward.

"Mia. Watch your language," Sara Callan admonishes.

"What's happening here?" Seth demands to know.

All of a sudden, Mia lurches toward me and pounds me as hard as she can. I'm at a loss for words when the nurses pull her off and take her to the locked, solitary, quiet room across the hall from the nurses' station.

"Tell me what the hell is happening here, young man," Seth orders again, but the nurses separate us, telling the Callans to leave before I can explain. The nurses take me to my room to sit down, hoping to stop my bloody nose.

While I was away from the room, a man in his thirties was sedated in front of me upon yelling that spiders were crawling all over him, and his bed replaced the former grandpa-aged, curmudgeon-type, overly vocal roommate with dementia. People come and go at the drop of a hat in here. It's a little scary at first, seeing someone's things just disappear, and the nurses can't tell you the specifics. It's almost like living in a horror story where they're recycling people who act up. Once the guy is knocked out, the nurses run across the hall to two patients fighting over a pair of hospital sock footies that both claim they own. A tussle ensues, and one of the nurses, the bald one, is punched in the head and gets both of those patients sedated—all that over a pair of socks.

"I'd give up the socks, man," I mumble to myself when a naked man streaks down the hall from the shower room. I cover my face and comb my fingers through my hair.

I go back out to the kitchen and read my book when Soraya asks if I'd play a game of Scrabble with her. Randy and Kerry, both alcoholics, brought in after detox, sit at the next table playing Clue.

Randy asks, "Why did Mia hit you, man?"

"She thought I told her parents some private information," I respond.

"What are you going to do with that private information?" Soraya prods.

I gave Soraya a glare that made her stop in her tracks. However, we were quite the adversaries at Scrabble, with scores in the three hundred, which is damn good for high school kids. Meanwhile, Kerry and Randy commiserated the whole time, forming a trauma bond.

While we sat there, two physical altercations happened, both times between older adults and about trivial stuff like closing curtains because it was lightning outside and what tv channel to watch, which was politically based, besides Mia and me, it was mainly adults who fought physically, which surprised me as I thought kids would misbehave more, but all in all, the fights weren't allowed to get out of control because the nurses jumped in pretty quickly. There are these two huge male nurses that I wouldn't want to go up against. They had fingers like sausages and no necks because they were so bulky.

We didn't get to finish our second Scrabble game because an overly medicated or wrongly medicated person tripped and grabbed our table, knocking the game board and distorting the tiles. That pissed me off because I was ahead that game. The brooding teen from therapy group helped us pick up the game pieces that slid off and tried to use that as justification that he played a game because his participation grade on the ward was low, and when that happens, you don't get released. Most teens on the ward have suicidal ideation, so we probably shouldn't be released too soon. It sucks because there is so much downtime and nothing to do but play card games or the few board games that belonged to the ward, which means not all the pieces are intact.

The next day, when it came time for pet therapy, I thought Mia would join us, but she was just being taken to be weighed due to her eating disorder. After that session, we signed up for art therapy, then horticultural therapy, where we got to go down to the greenhouse with one of the huge male nurses to accompany us and sit near the door. When we returned, both of our roommates disappeared again, and we were with adolescents with pronounced anxiety. My roommate has social anxiety so bad that they don't leave the room without being dragged or by a wheelchair and sedated. Soraya's roommate is clingy and fidgets constantly. It only took us about an hour to realize her roommate lied and was hospitalized for psychosis: she thought the devil was inside her and wanted her to kill people. It is a little disturbing how clingy she is.

"Can we talk?" Soraya asks.

"I suppose so," I respond, since there's nothing else to do, and I don't think her roommate will remember any of the conversations after they give her a hefty dose of an antipsychotic.

"What if they break into Mia's house again or do worse, like physically harm them?" Soraya asks. "Doesn't she have a kid brother?"

"I want to talk to Mia once to tell her that there was a break-in, so she understands why I'm breaking her confidence."

"There may not be time," Soraya deals us a hand of gin rummy.

"I know," I sputter and look around to see if Amy has come on shift yet. Amy is one of the younger nurses, but that doesn't mean she's a pushover because she works out and is in good condition; plus, she can get an attitude if riled up.

"There's Amy." Soraya points to the nurses' station.

I wait until the first opportunity that she comes onto the commons area and raise my hand like a foolish child, but she comes over and sits down with us.

"What's up, guys?" Amy asks.

"I need to tell you something about Mia," I cower a little.

"It's okay. You can share," Amy replies.

"Mia was raped at a party," I say.

"She told you this, or were you at the party?" Amy takes out a small notepad.

"No, I was in here and it was just before she was admitted."

"Okay," Amy continues to write, glancing at me for more information.

"Some older guys spiked her drink like we talked about the other day."

"And?"

"They took her upstairs and videotaped raping her."

"Has she told you this, too, Soraya?" Amy asks.

"No."

"Anyway, the early morning after, a girl from our teen depression group drove her home and threatened her."

"Threatened how?" Amy continues to write, not the least bit emotional, just a matter of fact, but interested.

"Brielle threatened Mia and her family with physical retaliation if she didn't go along with what they wanted her to do for the older guys at the party," I whisper so nobody else will hear.

"Do you know where this party was?"

"Yeah, Kira and Rory's house. Their parents weren't home. Kira and Rory are piano students of Mia's dad. He's a piano teacher," I explain.

"Does that mean that the bruises and bloodshot eyes that she displayed when she came in were due to the rape?"

"Yeah, and she never had the flu. It was due to whatever drug they laced her drink with that night."

"Why are you sharing this with me now? Do you mean to get back at her for hitting you?" Amy questions.

"No. When I saw Mia's parents, they told me that someone broke into their house and took a bunch of Mia's things, like her computers and stuff," I struggle to remember. My brain is getting a little foggy as I'm getting nauseous thinking about the gravity of what I'm doing to Mia. "The break-in targeted Mia's things with only a handful of other items of value taken from their home."

"This Brielle accomplice is in your therapy group?"

"Yes, she's about to turn eighteen, I believe."

"Did Mia go to the party alone?" Amy asks, which makes me mad at my buddy all over again.

"No, she went to the party with her best friend, Violet, and my best friend, Wyatt."

"What were they doing while Mia was raped?" she

asks.

"Mia said they were playing drinking games when she was taken upstairs. Then my buddy and hers thought that Violet took off and left them there, so they went home together, leaving Violet alone upstairs."

"Is there anything else?" Amy stares me straight in the eye.

"I don't think that I remember anything more than that."

"Okay. Well, obviously, Mia isn't going to be happy with you."

"I know," I respond, suddenly feeling an enormous weight on my chest. I think I'm having a panic attack or a possible seizure, so I put my arm to my chest and lean forward.

"Are you okay, Milo?" Amy asks.

"No, I'm having a difficult time breathing."

Amy tells me to stay seated while she holds on to me and yells for someone to get a wheelchair from the nurses' station, bringing out a couple more nurses.

"Milo, you did this for Mia. It is a good thing," Amy says.

She pushes me back to my room, where my socially anxious roommate bounces off the walls, worrying that I've got something contagious that will make him sick and die. The nurses warn him to calm down, but he just lies down in bed, pulls the covers over his head, and whimpers something incomprehensible.

"Please sit with him while I log some things in the charts," Amy tells one of the nurses.

I can barely breathe, and there's a heaviness about my chest that reminds me of the feeling Soraya said that she had after being given the spiked drink at the outdoor party. That, in turn, reminds me of my telling Mia. She's going to hate me. We'll never be friends again. That's the last thing that I remember after they gave me a muscle relaxant. I slept through a meal, but was allowed to go out to the dining area to get some fruit and a yogurt snack.

"Did they tell you?" Soraya approaches.

"Who? What?" I wonder.

"They must've asked Mia about it because she was uncontrollable. They'd brought her to her room, but she started kicking and yelling at them that they had sedated her and returned her to the quiet room." Soraya says.

"Holy crap," I respond.

"Then there was one police officer in the nurses' station. I'm uncertain as to whether or not that was about Mia."

"Oh, no. This spilling of information was a bad idea," I tell.

Just then, a phone call notification comes in for me over the intercom. I rush to take the call, excited to hear my mom's friendly voice, which will soothe my worries.

"Mom?" I answer.

"No. This is Seth Callan, Mia's dad."

"Yes, sir?"

"I'm very disappointed that you didn't tell us this information while we were in front of you the other night," Seth says, fuming.

"Sir, I tried, but then Mia attacked me when she saw me talking to you. I didn't say anything sooner because I didn't want to breach her trust."

"My family's life is in danger, and you're worried that you might lose a girlfriend?!" Mr. Callan yells.

"No. We're only friends. Or we were only friends at

the time," I explain.

"I will be contacting your parents immediately and alerting them of my disappointment. You and your brother should take lessons elsewhere," he says, then hangs up.

I pound my head into the phone bank wall. Soraya approaches to console me, but I gesture her away. I don't deserve comfort.

Mia

NOT WITH A BANG,
BUT A WHIMPER

I'm finally out of the quiet room with its two security cameras and padded walls. It's only because they needed it for an unruly foster kid who got kicked out of foster care and had nowhere to put her. I shouldn't judge, considering I've been in that quiet room for at least part of each day this last week. I'm still on my IV because I refuse to eat.

My new roommate has borderline personality disorder. She cycles through moods pretty quickly. One moment she is telling stories and laughing, dare I say almost dancing, then the next minute, she's balled up in her bed bawling. They have a nurse watching her for any possible suicide attempts.

At one point, I used our in-room bathroom, and the girl, Keri, shrieked violently. The nurse ran to her and then called for help. Apparently, she scratched herself bloody. They wrapped her hands tightly with medical tape and cleaned her wounds.

"Mia, you should come out to the dining room and eat something," Amy suggests.

"I don't want anything. And I don't want to see Milo," I stammered.

"He told us in order to we could help you and your family."

"Well, he should've talked to me about it first," I contend.

"You weren't speaking with him at the time," Amy makes a valid point.

"He shouldn't have told Soraya about me in the first place, which is why I was mad at him," I respond abruptly.

"But he didn't tell her. Milo asked questions for you, and she guessed what he was doing," Amy explains.

My roommate screams for her cell phone, which isn't allowed on the ward in order to respect everyone's privacy. No electronics that can record are permitted. Keri is infuriated.

"Mia, you need to come out of this room before we allow you to have visitors. Your parents desperately need to speak with you," Amy explains while Keri gnaws at her bandages. The other nurse calls for a sedative, which overly excites Keri to no end.

"What do they have to tell me? I'm sure they shared it with you already? The least you can do is entice me."

"I know they have some questions they need to ask you for insurance reasons to replace the stolen items from your bedroom," Amy elaborates on a few details.

Then there's an alarm that somebody broke loose through the emergency exits. Fortunately for the nurses, they don't allow street clothes, so he was in the bright orange hospital scrubs with grippy socks. Police apprehended him while he was trying to break into a house a few blocks away.

I sneak down the hall, pulling my IV along with me until I can see Milo and Soraya getting yogurt from the fridge. Their backs are to me, so they don't see me stalking him. I rush my IV back to my room, past the nurse doing suicide watch, and back to my bed.

"Mia, are you going to come out today or not?" Amy asks when she returns.

"She just slipped down the hall and back," the suicide watch nurse spills the beans.

"Really?" Amy is surprised. "What did you see?" she questions.

"Nothing," I reply. "Nobody."

Hours pass, and my roommate still has lethargic depression, so she's down for the count. I'm bored beyond tears. This stay traumatizes me more than anything. I'm learning to be afraid of all sorts of people, which is more judgmental than I was when admitted.

I want to talk to Milo, but I can't. I treated him like garbage to begin with because I'd been pissed off at the world for what happened to me at that party. Why did I take a drink from a stranger? I knew better. I was so stupid. I want to be mad at Violet and Wyatt, but can't seem to get rid of the self-blame.

"Mia, a policewoman, would like to speak with you. I can take you to the conference room near the nurses' station." Amy takes the IV tower and begins walking, and I follow beside her.

When we get to the dining area, I expect to see Milo and Soraya, but neither of them is anywhere to be found.

"Hello, Miss Callan, I'm Detective Korbel," A twenty-something tall female cop with long arms and fingers greets me in the conference room. She gestures for Amy and me to sit down. "Can I record this meeting?"

Once I say yes and we adjust the IV tower and take our seats, she sits and pushes over a statement form to write out. There are several pages of empty lines when I begin writing the cop and my nurse gab about the weather, an art fair, antique shops, working out on many exercise equipment, and taking fitness classes.

"Here you go," I push the forms back when I finish.

"Okay, Miss Callan, I have to ask you about what you filled out. Is that okay?" the policewoman queries.

"What time on the night in question did you leave for the party?"

"About 8:00 pm."

"What time did you arrive?"

"8:15 pm."

"Okay, I got the address here. And who did you go with? First names are good enough, as I see you spelled out their last names for me."

"Violet and Wyatt."

"Who greeted you at the party house?"

"Rory and Kira."

"What happened next?"

"Violet and Wyatt started playing some drinking games with Rory, Kira, Sadie, and some other younger kids."

"Why didn't you play with them?"

"Because I never drank before, and I didn't think that I could drink that fast to play the game."

"So, what did you do then?"

"I watched them from the side of the room."

"And then?"

"Danfield, this older guy, came over and gave me

some drink."

"What did Danfield look like?"

"Tall, blue eyes, dirty blonde hair, thick and wavy. He was very muscular."

"Was he good-looking?"

"I don't know. Yes, maybe?

"What kind of drink?"

"A soda because I kept refusing the drinks with alcohol in them."

"Why did you accept the drink?"

"Everyone else was drinking, and I just wanted something to drink to not stand out."

"What happened next?"

"Danfield and another guy talked to me about wild parties they'd attended in the past and different types of cocktails they've had."

"And then?"

"I remember them asking me about school. And then I was dizzy. My body felt heavier, and then we were walking up the stairs."

"Where were the others?"

"Playing games still."

"Did you go willingly?"

"No. I don't know. Yes, maybe?" I covered my mouth at the thought of it.

"It's okay. Now tell me what happened next?"

"I don't remember."

"When your memory returns, what is happening?"

"There's a camera at the foot of the bed. It's on a tripod. Danfield and Brielle are there. I realize that somehow I had sex because I felt pain in my crotch. I stood up but was dizzy and felt almost as if I had to vomit, so Brielle took me to the bathroom. Afterward, Danfield walked me down the stairs, and Brielle waited at the bottom. The other guy cleaned the bedroom, I think. He stayed behind."

"What next? Was anyone around?"

"Oh, Sadie came out of a different room upstairs but was grabbed by the hair and dragged inside?"

"By whom?"

"Danfield."

"I thought he was with you on the stairs."

"He helped me down the stairs, and I looked around, and when I turned around, he was gone, and then I saw him and Sadie upstairs. I think."

"Then what? Where were Rory and Kira?"

"I don't know."

"And your friends?"

"I don't know."

"So, what do you remember?"

"I got into a car with Brielle. It must not have been her car because it was a luxury model, something. I don't remember what kind of car it was, only that I puked in the front footwell."

"And then?"

"She drove me home but talked to me on the way."

"What did she say?"

"She said that I'd better listen to Danfield and the older guys, or they'll send my parents and everyone I know the pictures and video of how I had sex or something."

"I need you to be clear here."

"She said this isn't a game and that people get hurt. She asked if I wanted my parents or my brother to get hurt."

"Then?"

"I said no. Then Brielle said that when they contacted me, I better answer and do what they say."

"And?"

"Then she told me I'd better get back into my house without anyone noticing I'm gone, or Danfield would be upset with me. Then she dropped me off at home, and I went in the window of the powder room that faces our neighbor's house. Because I remember wondering if he was home to see me sneak into my house past curfew."

"What time was it then?"

"Around 3 am? I think?"

"You don't know?"

"No, I think I saw a clock somewhere. Maybe in the car? I can't be certain."

"Then what?"

"I puked and cried and showered. I was scared and disgusted. I wanted to get them off my skin."

"Who's them?"

"Anyone who touched me when I was asleep."

"Okay, Violet. I need to share some things with you, okay?"

"Yes."

"Rory and Kira know nothing about a party. Neither does Sadie nor Brielle. In fact, Brielle has an alibi. And we can't find a Danfield or any other older male that you said you saw."

"But?"

"Wait a minute," the policewoman holds her hand up.

"Violet and Wyatt said they took you to the party. But they didn't see any older guys there. They think that there might have been younger kids in the kitchen area. They said that you stood off to the side of the room for a brief while during their party games, then you took off on your own accord. They left together and made it home near curfew."

"What?" My face flushes uncontrollably. I'm devastated.

"Obviously, we have some youths who are lying. These are severe accusations."

"Oh, no. Damn, I knew that I shouldn't have told anybody what happened. Of course, something like this would happen to me," I'm bawling into my hands while the policewoman and my nurse respond emotionless.

"What's going to happen is we're going to continue to investigate this by talking to some of the neighbors, but Rory and Kira's house is a bit closed off from many of the neighbors as they have a large property out there."

"I take it back. I take it all back," I say and begin to stand, but the cop blocks the door.

"We aren't saying that you're lying. We're going to look into this further. You're right about a party. We just need to investigate further. Okay. Calm down. We also have the evidence of the break-in at your house, so we do think that something might have happened. To what extent and whose involved, we aren't certain. Let us do our job. Okay, Miss Callan?" The policewoman says and moves from where she stands, blocking the door.

I immediately rush out, pulling my IV tower, and head towards my room, feeling nauseous. Milo bumps into me by the phone bank.

"Mia?"

"Fuck off, Milo."

"Mia? What's wrong?"

"This is all your fault. You shouldn't have told anybody any of the things I shared with you in confidence. You're a jerk, Milo Chatham. And your friend over there, Soraya, is a slut. There. I said it. I hope you two are happy together. Don't ever speak to me again," I roll my IV tower down to my room.

When I return to my bed, I see that my roommate is medicated now but still has her nurse on suicide watch. But it's a different nurse now.

"Are you okay?" the nurse asks me.

"I'm fine. It's just that men are assholes."

"I know what you mean."

"Why do bad things happen to some people?" I toss it out there.

"Life happens. To everyone," she says.

"Especially me, though," I stutter.

"We all have messed-up lives. It's just to varying degrees," the suicide nurse says and then addresses my nurse, "Hello, Amy. Good to see you today."

"Hi, Dana," Amy says, then immediately looks at me. "Mia, nobody is accusing you of lying," she says calmly.

"Weren't you paying attention? He said somebody is lying?" I throw my arms in the air while bawling.

"I heard him say that it's unclear what happened and that there are different accounts of that party. Why do the party hosts claim that there was no such event? But your friends are on your side. Obviously, there was a party, right?" Amy sits on my bed.

I lean back against the headboard, sitting with my knees to my chest. "But Wyatt and Violet claim that there were no older men. That means they're saying I lied."

"It means they were focused on having a good time at the party and didn't concentrate on what you were doing. And I did hear that Violet and Wyatt thought other people were in the kitchen, but assumed they were younger, like Rory and Kira."

I open my covers and lie down in my bed. She massages my feet over the covers. I want to scream and cry, but all that remains is a grumble.

Milo

THE DEAD DON'T DANCE

Nurse Amy approaches Soraya and me during physical therapy in the gym. There's dance music playing, and we're supposed to limber up by stretching or dancing, whatever we feel like.

"Milo. Do you see Mia in the group today? This is her first time in a week. Maybe you'd like to welcome her and say hello or dance next to her?" Amy suggests that she stretch next to us at the front of the group of patients as we mimic the physical therapy facilitator.

"She considers me dead, nothing, nada," I stretch without looking back at Mia. Soraya remains quiet as she dances next to me.

"I don't think Mia meant what she said. She was just upset," Amy replies.

"Amy, I can't. She made me feel like crap. It hurt. Emotionally, I'm not there. I don't know if I'll ever be there again. I feel bad about what happened to Mia, but I can't make things better for her. I just amplify the bad," I stretch into Soraya's space, and we both laugh.

Mia sees Soraya and me touching momentarily, then giggling and tears off out the door as quickly as she's run from me for an entire week. Nothing has changed. Amy goes after Mia.

During the group exercise, we're still prompted to share and bond over similar experiences or mental health diagnosis symptoms. The physiotherapist walks around the room and assists those with lesser mobility. Meanwhile, our group of teenagers at the front talks and competes with those who can stretch the farthest safely. Soraya wins. She's the most limber.

"Just the participation can increase your internal drive to exercise more," says the physiotherapist helping an elderly man raise his legs from his wheelchair. "When you're answerable to a group, you get your peers' support, encouraging you to keep up with your recovery. It doesn't matter how much you can do; just being here aids your rehabilitation."

Afterward, Soraya and I go to the dining area to get some juice boxes when we see Mia toss her yogurt in the trash and stomp off to her room.

"I'm sorry that she feels bad, but I can't help her get better when she doesn't let me," I share with Soraya.

"No. I get where you're coming from. She has to take in what happened and come to the conclusion that you were only looking out for her best interest," Soraya responds.

"Yeah," I nod my head.

"Do you think that my being around you is making matters worse?" Soraya asks as she takes a break from drinking her juice box.

"No. This isn't you or me. This is about Mia now. She's going to have to step up and share or just say hello or anything," I brush the thought of Soraya making things worse out of the question.

"You're right. You can't help her get over it. She needs to invest in her own recovery," Soraya suggests.

"Thank you."

"You bet," she grabs the Scrabble game from the bookcase and returns to our table.

While we're playing, Randy and Kerry join us at the next table with their deck of cards.

"So, what's Mia's deal?" Randy asks.

"Just issues of her own," Soraya replies.

"Are you two like dating, Milo?" Kerry wonders.

"Not anymore," I respond, setting up my game tiles.

"I saw that policewoman in the conference room asking Mia questions. Then Mia took off, and the cop and the nurse came out and spoke of rape and spiked drinks," Randy shares.

Soraya and I glance in each other's direction, but try hard to avoid giving up the story.

"Isn't that what happened to you, Soraya?" Kerry asks.

"Yeah, it is. I don't know what Mia's story is, but I'm dealing with my past."

"So how do girls like get into sleeping with guys for money in the suburbs?" Randy questions Soraya outright. He stares at her until she answers him in detail.

"Much the same way it happens everywhere else."

"But kids in the suburbs have so much shit of their own already?" Kerry adds.

"Not all girls are so well off. Some want things they

can't afford working retail or at a restaurant. Then some are or were physically abused and misdirected in dealing with their trauma and get into situations they can't handle."

"Well, I guess that I never thought about that," Randy replies.

"Yeah, alcoholism made me self-centered. I didn't think to imagine others being abused. I mean, my dad kicked my ass, but thinking that it was also happening to others is the farthest thing from my mind. Do you know what I mean?" Kerry shares with all of us.

"I know what you mean," Randy acknowledges him.

"I think we're all so fucked up," Soraya says. "We've been that way for so long for different reasons that it's like we're on our own cloud floating through this world, and suddenly we realize there are other clouds, too," Soraya says. "But you know what I think?"

"What?" I bite.

"I think that we're going to be the ones that are better off having lived this shit and dealt with it through therapy," she adds.

"Do you think Mia will come through or will she fall through the cracks?" Kerry asks.

I drift off and think about Kerry's question. I hope that Mia doesn't fall through the cracks. She has to turn her life around and accept recovery. I couldn't bear to see her struggle too much longer. I wish she got what happened as Soraya did with her rape and subsequent feelings. By that, I mean that I hope Mia understands it wasn't her fault but tries to move forward and not wither. I fade back into the others' conversation.

"So, what are you two taking away from this psych ward visit?" I ask the boys.

"I'm going to try hard and stop drinking. It's going to be difficult because I'll have to give up my party friends."

"Kerry, I'm going to be your buddy. We'll do lots of shit like ultimate frisbee, workout at the community center, bike, or run on the trails."

"Yeah, Randy, but what will we do on weekend nights?"

"We'll order takeout, play video games, or catch a movie, and try to meet some girls. What do you think?" Randy responds.

"What do you think of AA? The nurses and the shrink want us to go," Kerry asks meagerly.

"Maybe if we can find a teen group. But I don't want to go with older people like those here; they're too depressing. I want to remain optimistic about my life."

"I know what you're talking about because it seems some of them have given up," Kerry replies while nodding.

"You guys could always try my depression therapy group since that's also your diagnosis," I share. "You too, Soraya?"

"Does Mia attend?"

"Twice."

"Then I don't think it is for me, Milo."

"Don't be silly. She probably won't even return," I respond.

"And, if you guys did want to attend an AA group, there's one for all ages that meets across the hall, but I've mainly seen twenty-somethings attend there," I suggest to the eager boys that nod their heads in response.

"So, Kerry, I think we might have a plan," Randy

smiles from ear to ear, as do the rest of us.

At that moment, Mia walks past and sees us all smiling and looking her way. She raises her middle finger to our group. All I can think is: Mia, what are you doing to yourself? You're just digging a hole to cower inside while the rest of us are just trying to get by.

"I think she pretty much hates you, man," Kerry says.

"Yeah, me too," I lean back in the chair, run my fingers through my hair, flatten and press my lips together.

It's only a matter of minutes before Mia returns, apparently from the phone bank. I bow my head and look away. I know what it's like to feel paranoid that people are talking about you with their friends, and hurting Mia is the last thing I want to do.

Mia

DEATH WEARS SQUEAKY SHOES

I just passed Milo and his crew in the dining area, where they are playing board games. They're all laughing at me. I just know it. Now Milo has another girlfriend, Soraya. She's a whore. He pretty much said so. Milo told me that her drink was spiked, and the men manipulated her into sleeping with men for money. Then she went rogue and did it on her own until a new crew appeared to manage her activities.

It pisses me off that Soraya is so pretty. She's petite, with long brown hair, big, beautiful eyes, perfect skin and nose, an enticing body, and an air about her that makes you want to get to know her. But not me. I'm not falling for that tramp. She can have Milo because I don't care anymore. It's not like we were really boyfriend and girlfriend, even though that was the status on our socials.

At supper time, I'll just sit on the opposite side of

the dining area from them, even though it will kill me to see them together. I dig my face into my pillow and scream. The observation nurse just stares at her patient. It's as if I don't exist. Why can't that be the case in general?

"Mia, do you want to fill out this paperwork now?" Amy brings in a clipboard holding the insurance paperwork my dad had dropped off and a pen, which isn't allowed unless with a nurse. My dad snapped pictures of my bedroom after the break-in, and now I need to list the missing items so that insurance can reimburse us.

"I just spoke to my parents, and they'll be up during visiting hours tonight," I tell.

"Yes, I heard when they called and asked for a status update on you."

"What did you tell them?" I cringe.

"I told them that you're improving, but there is still some animosity between you and another patient. They guessed that it was Milo." Amy says that she acknowledged that fact. She looks guilty, but I don't blame her.

"I hate him." I seethe.

"Because he told us about you? Or is it because he's friends with Soraya?" Amy hits the nail on the head.

"Why can't I stop thinking about him?" I say as I begin to cry.

"I think it's because you really care about him. I don't think he knows that with how you've treated him."

"I feel like they're laughing at me. I walked past them, and they all stared at me, smiling," I say.

"Maybe it was a welcoming smile? Have you thought about that? They're a nice group of kids."

"I just can't bear to be around them right now."

"Well, you'll have to be in the same groups as each other for the next few days at least.   Maybe the facilitator can help the whole group of you work things out once Milo recovers and returns to the young adult group. Shall I leave Resa a note?" Amy offers, but I shrug off her kindness.

"I don't think so," I mumble.

"Well, you're going to have to acknowledge him at some point. Why not in the safety of the group where an unbiased facilitator controls the group so things don't get out of hand and nobody gets hurt?"

"Maybe," I cave under pressure.

At supper, I get to the dining area early enough to get a seat all the way over by the window. Soraya enters first from that group and sees me. She waves. That bitch. Doesn't she know we're in a duel? Squeakers sound from down the hall, then Milo approaches the room. Milo sits down with his back to me, then suddenly turns around and waves as I look away. He tells Soraya and the nearby nurse that he left his slip-on sneakers too close to the shower. Apparently, he is going outside on a walk around the grounds after supper with that nearby nurse. The two other boys enter together and notice me. When they sit, one leans into Milo, who nods his head. What? Am I all they have to talk about?

About ten minutes into the meal, Milo collapses to the floor and starts having a seizure. The nurses surround him as my heart races, waiting minutes for him to come out of it, but he doesn't, and they're talking about a lack of breathing. They call a code, and at lightning pace, a rapid response team shows up, hooks a heart monitor to him, and finds him in V-fib.

They use the defibrillator, and the code team states they have a rhythm, but Milo remains motionless on the floor. I stand up and try to see, but get pushed back, where I tremble with fear of possibly losing him. A gurney rushes to his side, and he's loaded on, but I can't get a good look at what is happening. He's shrouded by nurses and doctors as they roll him down the hall and out of the ward. After he's taken away, the nurses work to settle everyone down. Amy stands beside me and holds my trembling fingers while I bawl again.

"You need to calm down, Mia," Amy says.

"Is he dead?" I ask.

"The team will work as hard as they can. We need to wait," Amy comforts and reminds me that I've got to eat something or the IV tower will return. I sit down and notice Soraya and the two boys staring at me.

After the meal is over for almost everybody but me, who eats slowly, Soraya and the boys approach my table, where Amy sits next to me to observe me finishing my meal.

"Hey, Mia, we just wanted to tell you that we hope that Milo is okay," Soraya says.

"Yeah, he's a tough guy. I'm sure he'll get through just fine," Randy is optimistic.

"Yeah, I agree," Kerry adds. "Hey, if you ever want to join us out here playing cards or board games, please just come take a seat."

"Yes, definitely," Soraya tosses in. They walk to the end of the hall with a charge nurse and a few other patients and wait to be buzzed out so they can access the elevators. Then the three of them leave to get ready for their walk around the hospital campus.

"What do you think of that?" Amy asks after they

leave.

"They didn't mean it," I sniffle.

"I think it took a lot for them to come over here and initiate the conversation. If I were you, I'd work on my social skills as it's obvious they want to befriend you. And that's probably because they know Milo feels similar," Amy stammers as she stares me down.

A rude old lady approaches Amy to ask for her meds, which need to be taken with her meal. The old woman mentions that I eat more slowly than she does. It makes me want to tell her that I have an eating disorder and that it's rude to call me out on my eating habits.

After supper, I eagerly wait to visit with my parents, who show up on time. I hug them tight as I see Milo's dad in the nurse's station. Amy came out to where we were standing to tell me that his dad said Milo was recovering from his seizure. That's all the information that she has at this time.

"Milo?" my dad fumes. "I told his father I don't want that boy anywhere near you."

"Dad, Milo collapsed into a seizure and was unresponsive. They used a defibrillator on him, and they rushed him to a different part of the hospital." I cry, and Mom hugs me.

"Oh, I'm sorry," Dad replies as he looks over at Milo's dad, who turns the other way.

"Dad, Milo was trying to maintain my trust as long as he could, then spilled the details in my best interest. Don't be mad at him, please?" I reach out for a hug.

"Sweetie, we could've been hurt or killed all the while he had the information," Dad stammers.

"I had the information, too. I didn't come forward. Hate me, not Milo," I beg.

"She's right, Seth." Mom acknowledges.

"But she was sick," Dad replies.

"So was he, Dad. Or he wouldn't be in here in the psych ward. He's fighting his own battles, and I shouldn't have placed mine for him to bear as well," I work to convince.

"I suppose you're right," Dad responds, looking over to Milo's father, who turns away again.

My parents and I spent the rest of the visiting hours sitting in the dining room, talking about how my brother is doing and the ordeal with the insurance company. While they talk, I notice Soraya's mom and dad look my way. That bitch told them about me. Isn't there any privacy anymore? When I walk my parents to the exit door, Soraya's parents follow close behind. After they all exit, I see Soraya's dad outstretched his hand to my dad. I watch as they talk. My mom puts her hand to cover her mouth and reaches out for Soraya's mom's arm. Then they hug. Shit. I knew Soraya had told her parents about me. Now they must commiserate with my mom and dad. Ugh.

Once back in my room, I wait for Amy to bring my evening meds, including a sleeping pill, so I don't have to be kept awake by my roommate's cries and rants, all the while still under observation. The nurses take turns sitting with her. It's weird to fall asleep with them simply staring across the room. I doze off with gratitude that they don't have to watch me all the time like my roommate.

In the morning, I awaken to be weighed down the hall across from the nurses' station. Then I shower and sit around waiting for breakfast, not because I'm hungry but to get it over with and get through the damn groups.

Fortunately, my eating disorder support group is my

first group of the day, so I won't have to see Soraya, Randy, or Kerry there. Instead, it's a couple of twenty-something females, a guy in his late teens, and a mom-type in her forties. They're all pretty friendly and talkative, which takes a lot of the social burden off of me.

"I'm Marcus, I'm gay, and I've got pica," he says.

"Would you like to share with the group what that means, Marcus?" Deidre, the facilitator, suggests.

"It means I eat paper, like new rolls of toilet paper, chalk, plaster, or sheetrock. It's a compulsion, and I've had it since I was about five. It is dangerous because I had a bowel obstruction once that totally freaked out my mom," Marcus shares.

"Who's next? The only one of you that I've seen before is Mia. So, Mia, would you like to share with the new patients what your eating disorder entails?" Deidre asks.

"I have bulimia, which means that I throw up what I eat to stay thin," I respond, hoping it suffices. I look to the new gals to suggest they share.

"Kathy, would you like to say something?" Deidre inquires the mom-type lady.

"I've got binge eating disorder, and it's like it sounds. I've had it since I was in my late teens. It's really troublesome because I waste a lot of money unnecessarily, which causes fights at home with my husband and sets a bad example for my daughter, who's about to graduate high school. I wish I could stop," Kathy cries, and I hand her the tissue box at my end table.

"I'm Traci, and I've got anorexia which means that I refuse to eat and am under surveillance here to get me to put on some weight which I'm not happy about."

"Same here. I'm Jami, and I can't stand eating. It's just a waste of my time. I could be exercising or working. I'm a freelance graphic designer, and I work from home. But I've started losing the strength to walk fast enough to keep up with my clients when I meet them at their places of business. It's mostly small businesses that I work for, and I worry my appearance will lose me some jobs in the near future. My parents brought me here when they found me collapsed on the floor. I told them I was fine, but they wanted to get me into an eating disorder clinic, but they're all full at the moment. I'm on a waiting list."

Then Deidre proceeds to ask why we think we have eating disorders. Marcus and Jami answer in unison that it's control issues. The three of them go on to delve deeper and find that for them, it was the result of sexual abuse as a child, which they never got over, and found that their eating disorder allowed them control over their lives, unlike their lack of power as a kid being abused.

Traci pipes in that her parents' divorce brought on her eating disorder, at which time Kathy chimes in. That is when hers started as well. They both needed control of their situation.

When Deidre looks at me, I add, "That's similar to my case, where my parents were fighting, and their affairs brought on my bulimia and overexercising."

Overall, it was a pretty good group, much better than what I've got to look forward to in the young adult group this afternoon, or quite possibly the depression support group where Soraya, Randy, and Kelly will all be present. I sigh and think about how Milo is doing.

Milo

DAMN YOU ANYWAY

Why can't I get you off my mind, Mia Callan? Especially after the way that you've treated me, I'm still thinking about you. But you piss me off as I sit here on the other end of the hospital waiting to be transferred from the cardiac ICU to the medical-surgical unit and back to the psych ward. I both can't wait to see you and don't want to endure your attitude simultaneously.

Upon discharge from the medical-surgical unit, a psych nurse brings my wheelchair, which I'll remain in for the next few days. The doctors didn't find anything wrong with my heart and instead focused on the initial seizure. I did get six stitches for my head wound, though. They shaved a little bit of my hair to do it.

I adjust my shaved spot by pulling some adjacent hair over to cover it. "Does it look horrendous?" I ask the nurse transferring me back to the psych ward.

"Not at all. Plus, you have a good reason," the nurse responds.

"Yeah, but I'm just in time for the young adult support group, and there are people in there that I'd like to look good for, you know?"

"Milo, you look fine," she says, pushing me through the buzzing door at the end of the psych ward hallway and down to the group therapy room.

"Hey, guys," I say to Soraya, Randy, and Kerry as the nurse pushes me into place next to Soraya on the far side of the sofa, next to the facilitator's chair at the front. Resa isn't in her spot yet. I look around and don't see Mia yet, either.

"So, what happened?" Randy asks.

"Well, after the seizure, they said I had developed a heart arrhythmia, meaning my heart wasn't beating properly. It didn't do much damage, so as long as I'm still in the hospital and in this wheelchair and not overexerting myself. They gave up that bed to someone who needed it more than me. So, I'm back here with you guys," I say, noticing through the glass wall that Resa and Mia are about to enter together.

"Okay, teens, nurse Amy brought up a special request to start this group session. Apparently, a handful of you are seemingly at odds with each other, and we need to deal with it here and now."

I'm confused and look to Soraya and the guys, who shrug their shoulders at me. Then I look to Mia, who lowers her head, and I realize this discussion will involve her and probably me and maybe Soraya and the guys.

"So, Milo, I realize you just returned from the medical unit. I don't want to seemingly pick on you, but is there a problem with you and Mia that I can help address today?" Resa questions.

"I'm a little thrown off, but yeah, we're not talking

because Mia is upset with me," I state matter-of-factly.

"I'm not mad at you," Mia responds.

"Well, giving me the finger because I looked at you seemed like a sign."

"I was just caught off guard at that moment with you and your friends all staring at me when I walked by, and you were all smiling like you guys were all in on a joke," Mia wipes tears from her eyes.

"Not at all. We just happened to look up at the moment you walked by, and if we were all smiling, it was because of what was said just previously that I, for the life of me, cannot remember at this moment," I reply and look to Soraya and the guys.

Randy chimes in, "Yeah, we'd been laughing, but I can't remember why. It seems so unimportant now, but it wasn't about you."

Kerry adds, "I don't remember either, but no, it wasn't about you."

Soraya hesitates, then stutters, "And Milo and I are just friends. I knew you guys were dating. I wasn't stepping on anyone's toes. You seemed very upset with me, too."

"No. I don't care if Milo's got new friends," Mia snaps.

"Okay, Mia, what you just said may be hurtful, curt, and misconstrued. You don't want Milo to think that you don't care about him because that's what I just heard from you," Resa asks.

"I mean, I care about you, Milo. I just wasn't upset that you had new friends of your own in here," Mia clarifies.

Kerry notes, "We're not just Milo's friends. We're open to friendship with you, too, Mia. I think Randy and Soraya feel the same way, right?"

Soraya nods enthusiastically, "Definitely, Mia."

"You bet, Mia," Randy tidies that up.

"Okay, now Amy noted that there is some misunderstanding about how the information got relayed about something that happened to you, Mia. Is that the case, everyone?" Resa wonders, holding up the note from nurse Amy and scanning it front and back.

"I didn't tell Soraya about you, Mia," I breach the subject.

"No, he didn't. He was asking me questions about my experience, and then I asked if he was asking for you, and I said your name, and there you were in front of me. He never told me a thing. But when you ran off, I just sort of came to that conclusion on my own," Soraya explains to Mia directly.

"And Mia, when I heard about the break-in at your house, I worried your brother or parents could be in danger and not know it. At that time, you weren't speaking to me, so I couldn't ask you if I could break your confidence, so I had to take the chance for your family's safety."

"Okay, thank you all for clarifying for me. I'm sorry I was upset with all of you, especially you, Milo," Mia says.

"Are we okay, now? I mean everybody. Soraya's just a friend, and I'm sure she'd be a pretty good one to you as well," I strongly suggest.

"Okay, is everyone okay now? Have we cleared up all the loose ends?" Resa asks, taking notes on the letter from nurse Amy. "Good. Has anyone else got anything to say on this matter? Or are we done?"

"Yeah, what the hell is going on? It sounds like serious shit went down, and I'm an outsider here. It's like you guys are talking in code or something?" the brooding teen from the previous sessions speaks up, and a couple of other new teens nod their heads in agreement.

Resa looks around and is about to say something when Mia spiels out of the blue, "I was at a party, my drink was spiked, and I was raped. I had thought that Milo was telling everyone about me." She says, then lowers her head.

"Holy crap, I had no idea. Wow. Are you okay, or is that why you're here?" the brooding teen asks.

"I have some post-traumatic stress that I'm working on along with my depression and an eating disorder, but I'm fine at this moment. Thank you."

"And the same thing had happened to me, which is what I was telling Milo when I guessed that it happened to Mia when she appeared and heard her name, thinking Milo was telling me about her," Soraya adds.

Randy and Kerry look shocked and turn to each other with their mouths open, then gain composure and reconnect with the group's dynamic.

"Wow. I've only heard stories about stuff like this happening at parties. I'm surprised and feel bad for both of you," says a new girl. "I'm Amanda, by the way."

"I'm Gabi," adds the other girl.

"I'm Ethan," says the brooding teen.

"Well, good. I'm very pleased to see things open up here. Since we're on this subject, let's talk about it and put off my planned topic until tomorrow," Resa sets down her clipboard. "What advice does anyone have for taking care of themselves or others at parties?"

"Well, don't go to a party alone, which is pretty much what happened to me since my friends ditched me to play drinking games once we'd arrived at the party," Mia shares.

"And don't accept drinks from anyone you don't know, from any gender. The girls may be working for the guys and try to slip you drugs," Soraya relays.

"Yeah, I hear that some bartenders try to make an extra buck by slipping pills into someone's drink for a buddy of theirs. So just plain don't take drinks that you don't see poured right in front of you from the original bottle," Gabi adds.

"And guys, how can you help the spiked drink situation when you're at parties?" Resa looks around the room.

"Well, don't leave your date alone," Randy offers.

"Watch out for others that this may be happening to and warn them," Kerry follows up shortly after Randy, and there was a pause in the room where you could hear a pin drop.

"And if it does happen to you, call 911 from where you wake up and don't shower or anything," Soraya suggests.

"This is good stuff, guys," Resa looks through the glass wall to the hallway where another group across the hall lets out. She looks up at the clock and says, "Well, that ends our meeting today. Sorry that I was a bit late to start. I'm very pleased. And good sharing on everyone's part." Resa stands up and makes her way to the doorway.

Everyone else gets up to leave when Randy asks if he can help with the wheelchair. I look to Mia, who is going fairly slowly to leave.

"No, I think I got it, Randy. Thanks, you go on ahead," I say.

Soraya looks at me, then Mia, and excuses herself, too.

"Milo, I'm so sorry," Mia stays behind with a flushed face.

"It's all okay now, right?" I ask. "Could you get the door for me, please?"

We hang back from the crowd as we walk down the hallway to get a juice box before our next group, which will focus on depression. The others rush to their rooms to use the restroom. Once everybody is back in the junction between the gender-specific corridors, near the nurses' station, we head back down to the larger of the group therapy rooms to meet up with the adults who are also diagnosed with depression.

Lily and Jack facilitate that group and are already in there waiting for the room to fill in. Once it does, they focus on how to deal with rejection without allowing it to override their lives.

"What are some times that you may feel rejected?" Jack asks while Lily takes notes on the marker board.

"At work," someone in the back yells.

"With a boyfriend," Gabi says.

"Ghosting by a girl," Randy adds.

"By your parents," Kerry grimaces.

"Peers," Mia says.

"Okay, now what are the feelings associated with the rejection?" Lily asks and prepares to write.

"Sadness," Soraya offers.

"Emptiness," Kerry lowers his head.

"Heartache," Amanda adds.

"Physical aches," mom-type Kathy says.

"And what can we do about our feelings that don't have us adding to our depression? Jack looks around the room. He points to Marcus.

"Listen to my music," Marcus shares.

Jami adds, "Go for a walk in nature or even just sit

out on your patio or deck. Get some sunlight on your skin. Feel the warmth."

"Draw or sketch," I put out there. "Maybe build something."

"Play with your dog or cuddle the cat," Kathy offers.

"Maybe go for a drive," Traci suggests.

"Watch a comedy movie," Jami says. "But then again, when I stream too many movies in a row, it makes me more depressed. So, I don't know."

"You've got a point there, Jami," Jack acknowledges.

"Cooking or cleaning," Amanda smiles, "Sometimes I scrub and scour my apartment from top to bottom. I'll shower, and then I'll make a fancy dish for myself like a small vegetable lasagna or baked ziti with garlic bread."

"Yeah, but doesn't eating alone get you more down?" Gabi wonders.

"Read a book or magazine at the bookstore or a library?" Mia offers.

"You guys have me stymied," Randy grimaces, "Just keeping up with the basic functions of life like eating and personal hygiene are insurmountable when I'm depressed. I don't know. Maybe my depression is worse?"

Everyone smiles, and almost everyone shakes their head in his direction.

"Okay, then maybe play some video games," Randy stammers.

"Now see, that would make me depressed if I had to do it alone," Traci responds.

"What about talking to a therapist, using crayons in a coloring book, reading comics, video chat with a faraway relative?" Lily suggests and marks on the board.

"The point is," says Jack, "there are numerous things we can do to occupy our time when we're depressed. Try not to let the rejection get you down, and you're right, Randy; when severely depressed, that may be the time to schedule an appointment with your therapist or psychiatrist to check the status of your meds."

Lily adds, "Maybe journal too, so you can better keep track of your moods, and when you feel a tough time coming on, you can schedule those appointments that Jack referred to."

"I agree with Randy. You can do these things if you're rejected and down in the dumps. When I have severe depression, my body aches, I'm lethargic, have no appetite, and almost no will to live," Amanda shares.

"I hurt myself when I'm depressed and can't bear to cope," Mia says, and the room acknowledges her.

"That's when you tell a loved one, and they can bring you to your therapist, doctor, or hospital. Again, it may be as simple as a medication change, or you may need some downtime in here with us," Jack states. "The point is, don't go it alone."

When group time is up, the room empties in little cliques, of which Mia is now a part of ours. She pauses to get behind my wheelchair and push me out into the dining room, where Soraya, Mia, and I play a game of Clue while Randy, Kerry, and Ethan play poker. My depression already feels like it's lifting.

Mia

CASTLES IN THE CLOUDS

Things in the psych ward at 4 North are working out wonderfully. Yes, I still have nightmares and post-traumatic stress in addition to the depression and my eating disorder, which will probably be lifelong. But now that things are cleared up with Milo, Soraya, and the guys, it's more bearable in here, if not downright boring. We spend a few hours a day in therapy, and the rest of the downtime is spent playing cards or board games in the dining area. I feel bad for the others, especially the older ones, who just sit around and wait for a meal or a visit from family, if they have any.

When visiting time comes around, Milo and I take the opportunity to bring our parents together to solve the dispute over the miscommunications. In the end, Dad welcomes Milo and Beckett back as his piano students, and the Chatham's say I'm welcome to their house to see Milo anytime.

After Milo's family leaves, my mom and dad welcome Soraya's parents, who talk as we sit quietly beside them.

"You need to keep hounding the police department," her dad insists.

"Don't take no for an answer," her mom warns, making my mother tremble.

"How do we go about locating this young rapist to make him face the consequences?" my dad wonders. "I had a friend set up a social media account online and reeled the guy in," her dad continues. "Everything was recorded, and the guy was sent away to jail for a few years to learn his lesson," he says, puffing his chest. "The key was never to have the prey initiate the sexual conversation, suggest sex, or meet. A societal good is served by identifying and arresting this pedophile who is actively looking for girls to exploit."

After our parents leave, Soraya approaches me to share how intense and frightening that conversation we just listened to truly was for her.

"How are you, Mia. I mean, with the sexual assault?" Soraya asks.

"I'm anxious, and a similar guy's hair, muscles, nose, or hands trigger panic. At night, I get out of my bed and sleep on the floor because the unfamiliar bed reminds me of that place where it happened," I explain as tears stream down my face. "And it feels like hands are all over me, touching me, making me nauseous."

"For me, it's smells or sounds of a certain type of laughter, and I hate people touching me. I don't know if I'm ever going to get over that and be able to have a real relationship. It scares me to be alone, and I worry if that's how it will always be," Soraya explains.

"How did you feel in order to continue doing it

even after the perpetrators went to jail?" I say then, worrying I may have hurt her feelings.

"Good question. I felt like trash and didn't deserve anything good, only bad things, which the men definitely were. Some of them beat me, and I almost felt better afterward because I was so brainwashed that I deserved to be hurt and humiliated."

"That's terrible."

"I told myself that I was doing it for the money, but my parents are well off and gave me everything I needed. No. I only did it to feel like garbage during and numb afterward," Soraya finishes. "We'll talk more tomorrow. Goodnight, Mia."

I stand there alone and watch the ward's common areas empty out. Amy comes over to me and asks me why I'm not in bed.

"I'm afraid to lie down because I'll imagine him on top of me, but that's strange because I was unconscious when the sex happened. That's messed up, right?"

"You are right to feel any way you want. That's up to you. And it's also up to you to change it and take power back. He's long gone. Don't give him that power over you. Now we need to get you to bed. I'll get your sleeping pill," Amy says.

Early the following day, they woke my new roommate and me to be weighed. She also has an eating disorder, and it surprises me to find Milo walking down the hall towards me, where we meet in the commons area.

"I knew they wake you early for weigh-in. I thought if you couldn't get back to sleep, we could sit and play gin rummy or read near each other," Milo says. Damn, he's handsome and so considerate. I feel guilty for mistreating him.

As we sit there across the table from each other, reading novels: his science fiction and mine, a classic that is a requirement of my homeschool curriculum, we accidentally bump feet. I feel weird—an immediate surge of attraction to Milo, then repulsion to a male. I rush to the bathroom to vomit.

Afterward, I curl into a fetal position on the floor, where Amy finds me and helps me to bed, but I can't lie down. I sit and bawl that I embarrassed myself in front of Milo.

"If he cares about you, then you can't make a fool out of yourself in front of him. Don't be embarrassed. Just go out and explain what happened."

When I get out to the dining room, Soraya sits next to Milo but smiles sincerely when I approach them.

"Good morning, Mia," Soraya says. "I hear that you're under the weather."

"No. Soraya, I'm messed up. What happened was that Mio's feet and mine touched, and there was an attraction and a repulsion. Tell me that I'm going to get over this, please," I cry, and Soraya stands up to hug me.

"In due time, but it's all so recent to you. You're still grieving your loss to that rapist. Maybe when they catch him, things will be better for your relationship," she says, then looks to Milo. "Meanwhile, you'll be patient, right?"

"Of course. I'm sorry, Mia." Milo says, which makes me feel guilty, but I don't want to drag out the situation. I want to forget about it.

I find it comforting that Soraya sits with us. It's as if there's a buffer between any romantic connection that will make me nauseous. When it's time for breakfast, the guys join us. Now that includes Ethan, too. Afterward, they get board games out while I head to my eating disorder support group.

"Come on in and sit down," Deidre gestures to everyone to hurry. "It's just that time goes by so quickly, and I want to give everyone a chance to share."

"What's our topic today?" Jami asks while we find our seats.

"Abuse. It can be physical, sexual, or emotional. Words hurt, too," Deidre explains.

"Well, that's easy: sexual abuse when I was a child," mom-type Kathy responds rather assertively. "It was my father, then my stepfather, and a couple of guys that stayed late after my mom and stepdad fell asleep after bringing people home from barhopping. I've come to terms with it and talked about it in therapy for years, but the memories continue to knock me on my ass; I drank myself near dead a couple of times to quell the psychological pain. It doesn't go away. It finds me when I wash dishes, vacuum, or clean the oven. And I just break down and grab a bottle of wine, cocktails, liquor, pretty much anything I can get my hands on."

"Ditto," adds Marcus. "An uncle sexually abused me for about four years until I broke down and told my mom. It was her brother. I've always had the sense that she blamed me. She's still close with him, which makes me think she either blames me or doesn't believe me. I asked her once, and she said that he apologized to me for what I said happened. It was how she said it, though: 'what I said happened' like it was made up, and my well-meaning uncle took the bullet to help me get through it all. Do you know what I mean?" Marcus looks around the room, and we all nod.

"For me, it was my assistant coach," says Jami. "I

was goofing off, so he made me stay late and run some laps; afterward, I was taking a shower when he joined me. He told me that nobody would believe me as opposed to him. I knew that he was right. After all, he was a family man with a new wife and a brand new baby that he showed everyone pictures of because he was such a good and proud dad.

The group looks at me, and I lower my head and say, "My drink was spiked at a party. I don't remember having sex, but it was videotaped, and I can't prove that it happened."

Traci says, "Mine was date rape. He was the sweetest guy. I never would've imagined what happened that night. We had a nice dinner and a movie, where we held hands while we watched a couple of toddlers running around in a circle. He pointed it out and said how cute it was. Once in his car, he started telling me about his mom and sisters and how close he was to them. He seemed very family-oriented. So, when he asked if we could go to a sports bar and get some drinks, I nodded, and we were off laughing and telling funny family stories. Then, after a few cocktails, I felt woozy and asked him to take me home, but he didn't. He took me to a park and said we should get in the back seat so we could just make out a little. I was up for it, but that was all. In the end, it was my word against his. He was convicted, though, served ninety days, and was put on probation for three years, which I feel was a joke."

It is weird that we all share such difficult stories, but none of us cry. Instead, the others look lost. Maybe I do as well. Is that what we've become, lost souls? I don't want to give that asshole that power. I drift back from my thoughts to what they're talking about in the group at the moment.

"How is the initial sexual violation exacerbated?" Deidre asks.

"People think I'm promiscuous and say things within earshot. You're right that words hurt like a son of a bitch. I used to counter their accusations at first, but then decided to let them think what they want," Traci says.

Kathy adds, "Well, they call me a lush because I can't hold my liquor. I can hold my liquor, but I don't want to because I want to drown the damn pain."

"I don't think I can or worry that I won't be able to have a physical relationship again," I admit while tears stream down my cheeks. "My rapist took the enjoyment away. Is it going to be that way forever?" I ask.

Marcus and Jami nod their heads. I lean forward and bawl. Traci slides down the couch and holds me in her arms while I cry. When I look up, everyone, even Deidre, sheds tears. We all sit there crying until we laugh about how emotional we are.

"Emotions are a good thing. It shows you're still living, breathing, getting up daily, and fighting for your life back. Therapy takes time. It isn't easy, but we do it. We're fighters," Deidre reveals.

After the group, I walk down the hall and see Milo, who notices my red eyes and me wiping my red nose. He stops in place and looks like he's about to cry. He looks up and away, but I approach him. I call his name, and at first he doesn't look at me, but when he does, I see that he's crying, too. Even though it's against the psych ward rules, I reach over and hug him tight and promise him that I'm going to battle this the best I can, so I don't lose him.

"Not a chance in hell," Milo replies.

I look around the ward and see people who have become true friends, not the superficial kind, but deep, well-meaning people who will give you the shirt off their back to shield you from the elements. I wipe the tears from my eyes and pull back from Milo.

"Believe it or not, I'm happier here than I am at home. I know it's going to take a lot of therapy, but I'm going to manage this the best I can," I say.

Milo

BORROWING TIME

Our insurance companies took a few weeks to kick us out of the psych ward and back home to deal with our pains in private. Sure, they'll continue to pay for therapy, just not top dollar, which is what hospital care costs.

I was released two days before Mia. The others all went before us, but we connected on socials immediately but hid our list of friends from prying eyes or making our accounts private. And it was Randy and Kerry that came up with a way to find Danfield for Mia's case.

Ethan, Randy, and Kerry would take turns following Brielle until she meets up with someone matching Mia's description of her rapist. The time they're committing to this mission is inspiring.

Mia and I continue to attend the young adult depression support group at the clinic. Randy, Ethan, and Kerry attend the AA group across the hall. Brielle, Rory, and Kira join intermittently and sit as far away as possible. Jessica Walsh is a therapist to us all, so she can't take sides, but she's aware of Mia's accusations against Brielle, Rory, and Kira.

Every group meeting is intense. Take tonight, for example; after Jessica started the group, Mia began to share when Kira coughed and got Mia's attention. If looks could kill. Wow. Kira ended up crying and running out of the room with her twin on her tail.

At school, I made it known to everybody that Brielle, Rory, and Kira have a hand in helping to spike drinks. Since then, the trio has skipped a third of their classes. People are talking.

Tonight, Brielle is holding out longer than I expected her to. She's really standing her ground in the group. She's alert with attitude. So, it comes as a surprise to me that Ethan, Randy, and Kerry can pull the wool over her eyes and follow her around the community after groups let out. And just as we've hoped, she took them to a small shack of a house the next suburb over, where Ethan gets out to hide in the bushes and peek inside to verify Danfield's residence. Once we have him, we don't need Brielle, but having her arrested in addition to Danfield will only be icing on the cake.

"Milo, we got his address. He's in there with a couple of other guys. There's shit everywhere. Are they like in a shoplifting ring or what? There's a bunch of computers, what appears to be unopened boxes of electronics stacked up against the wall, and trays full of jewelry. It's weird," Ethan whispers.

Someone looks in Ethan's direction, and he makes himself scarce. We agree to follow Danfield another night, quite possibly this weekend.

"What's his address?" Mia demands to know.

"No, I'm not telling you because you'll go there or do something dangerous. I won't let you get hurt," I respond angrily to Mia.

"I'm not going to go there. I'm going to scour the dark web for his first name and home address, get as much data on him as possible, and fuck him up," Mia practically growled. "Thankfully, he has an unusual first name."

"Okay. But I'm trusting you don't go anywhere near him," I say.

"Promise," Mia replies.

And in short order, she has his listings for all his new products at his online marketplace, which is attached to a payment account that she breaches and returns all the payments he's received in the last thirty days. Mia then hacks his bank accounts and donates the balances to charities.

"Won't he guess that it's you, since he has your computers at his place?" I ask Mia.

"Not a chance someone like him can break my password. He's too stupid. Danfield is nothing but a thug," Mia replies.

I ask her if I can kiss her goodnight on the cheek, and she nods, takes my hand in hers, and squeezes.

We're pretty proud of ourselves, so we settle in for the night and wait for the weekend.

After I bike home, my mom makes me some tea and brings it to my workshop, where I'm struggling to keep up with the orders that didn't stop while I was in the hospital.

"Mom, that'll just put me to sleep," I push it away and grab a soda from my beverage fridge near the back door when I see a shadow pass by outside. Upon looking at security footage, I see the figure of a female in a hoodie. I conclude it's Brielle but keep that from my parents and the police officers who arrive. However, I tell the police to warn the Callans because it may be related to my friendship with Mia.

Now that the weekend has arrived, Ethan, Randy, and Kerry coordinate tracking Danfield from his home to any party that Danfield has planned. They are texting me their every movement. It's not until 8:00 pm that there's any activity. Randy follows a few cars behind Danfield to a burger joint, a gas station, and a vape shop.

Finally, they're on the road and heading to a gated community on the west side of our rather good size suburb. There's a line of cars waiting for the security guard to let them in. Randy passes the gated entrance, parks his car down the street, rushes to the light rail trail that intercuts the gated community, and climbs the fence. Once Randy's over, he jogs down the street where he sees Danfield's car head up the small hill to a more sparse street and finally the more secluded stately home at the end of the road. Randy slips between some bushes to call the other guys.

Within an hour, Ethan and Kerry make their way to Randy's phone, which they put a tracker on prior to the covert operation. They lay low in thick landscaping surrounding the modern, white geometric tri-level, gallery-like estate until other cars arrive, which fortunately comes after the cover of darkness. First, they see Brielle's beat-up, older sedan, then a few other luxury vehicles, mainly SUVs, with a bevy of teen girls screeching, laughing, and hollering with beer bottles in their hands.

Maple, juniper, and birch trees shroud the contemporary home from its nearest neighbors a few hundred feet away, which are cloaked in grand oaks and maples of their own design. Noise spills onto the expansive backyard with its multi-level deck, industrial-looking railing, and terraced landscaping encircles the circumference of the bright azure-colored pool. Nearby, off the center of the grey concrete patio, its outdoor kitchen and fully-catered dining area entice the lighted display, which can be seen from the ample seating arrangements throughout with their own small firepit areas.

Ethan videotapes from his blanket of grass behind a swath of tall prairie grasses blowing in the wind. He watches Danfield, and two other guys watch raccoons scurry the lighted pathways throughout the rear landscape. Randy and Kerry are enveloped in a throng of hydrangeas as they watch the flock of teen girls undress near the hot tub, an extension of the lighted home gym. Kerry scans the surrounding area of the sloping hill, then a gentle drop in grade that leads to the gated community's surrounding swath of oak trees just before the walking trail and distant highway.

One of the guys sets up camp at the bar space of the outdoor kitchen. Danfield gestures the okay sign, and Ethan zooms in to film the bulky, tall dude spiking drinks with crushed pills from the mortar and pestle to his side. The other stocky guy loads the drinks onto a tray which he hastily carries to Danfield and the young girls.

Brielle can be seen through the windows of glass walls and the bedrooms above. In two bedrooms, she's setting up camera equipment on tripods surrounding the beds. She adjusts portable camera lighting to focus on the bed from different angles.

Randy whispers to Kerry that he should now call the police since the girls have just been handed their drinks. But the call takes a bit, and the light from Kerry's phone garners the attention of the bartending guy in the outdoor kitchen, who yells and waves violently to Danfield, who just entered the hot tub with the girls now tasting their spiked drinks. The bartender tears off in Randy and Ethan's direction with the stocky server in tow.

Danfield rushes out of the hot tub and takes two steps at a time up to the bedrooms, where he has Brielle speedily tear down the camera equipment while he gathers his clothes from the master bedroom's sitting area chairs. Then Danfield grabs what cameras he can carry and hurriedly descends the interior stairs and out the front door.

The girls in the hot tub are none the wiser and continue to drink their spiked cocktails, all the while hooting and hollering for the guys to return. Meanwhile, Randy and Kerry sprint down the gated community's streets with a rapidly approaching bartender on their tail. Just as he's about to take down the guys that are running for their lives, Danfield pulls up alongside the bartender, who jumps into Danfield's vehicle. They back the car up and get the stocky server whose out of breath and back one block.

Ethan stands up to reveal himself to the girls while continuing to film, and all the while screaming, "Stop drinking. The drinks are spiked," but the loud music surrounding them prevents them from hearing a thing." The girls wave to the camera and dance to the music until one girl starts to climb out of the hot tub feeling woozy. Then another girl exits in a dizzy dance to dry off at the outdoor shower's towel hooks.

Just then, Brielle tears out of the driveway and down the street. Police pass her by and descend onto the circular driveway and courtyard at the front of the estate. Police officers rush to the see-through building to get to the back patio, where girls are suddenly collapsing onto the concrete patio. Ethan nervously backs up and calls the police station to alert them to his presence because he's scared of the officers on the scene pulling guns on him. In a matter of minutes and over-the-shoulder radios, they learn of Ethan, Randy, and Kerry. They are now standing with their hands in the air and approaching the rear over-lit walkways that lead to the central concrete patio where paramedics arrive to help the passed-out trio of girls. The other two only sipped their drinks once and aren't fully intoxication.

Randy, Kerry, and Ethan are searched and taken into custody along with their cameras and phones. Only after hours of interrogation and the police watching the videos are they released. The address they gave to the police to find Danfield and the others was empty, but they confiscated all the stolen equipment they found.

I get the call from Ethan at the police station and round up my parents as well as Mia's parents, who drive us down there to explain. Once Mia sees the captured image of Danfield from the videotape, she IDs him as her rapist and Brielle as the accomplice. The operation did not go as planned because three innocent girls were still poisoned but are recovering at the hospital. And Danfield is nowhere to be found. Neither is Brielle, but the police are at least searching for them. Mia's case has been put back near the top of the pile, thankfully, because it's empowered her to seek justice and take away Danfield's power over her.

Mia

BREATHING HALLELUJAH

Violet is arriving. I greet her at the door, and she follows me up to my bedroom with tears streaming down her cheeks.

"Mia, I had no idea what you went through. I'm so sorry," Violet apologizes and reaches out to hug me, but I back away.

"I can't do this. Not yet, anyway," I say. "Let's fix our friendship slowly, okay?"

"Of course. Any way you want to work things out is fine with me," Violet agrees. "I was an ass that night. I should've stayed by your side. And Kira. That bitch. She lied about even having a party. I was so furious with her and her brother."

"They got in trouble for their actions. I don't know how much good it will do because her dad is a lawyer. But maybe he'll stand up to his kids and stop enabling them," I explain.

"So, are Wyatt and Milo going to run with us today? Where will we go?" Violet asks while stretching on my bedroom floor.

"They are working on their friendship as well. Milo is talking to Wyatt as we speak, and then they'll be over in like twenty minutes, I think," I answer her while stretching on the opposite side of the bed.

"Did they find Danfield yet?"

"No. But it's only a matter of time. At least now the police and everyone else knows he exists and the fact that Brielle was his accomplice," I tell. "At first, I was scared of him, but now that I know how much support I have behind me, it's more manageable, plus I'm going to therapy a lot."

"How is the eating disorder and the depression?" Violet asks, jogging my memory back to the middle of last night.

I woke up screaming, flailing about with fear so intense it hurt to breathe. Mom rushed in first, and Dad shortly after to get the washcloths that Mom used to wipe the sweat off my face and neck. I had no memory of what I was just having a nightmare about. It was just an intense sadness, loneliness, and despair. Insanity worried me. What if I tear off all my clothes and run down the street naked? Mom said not to worry, that won't happen. But the night terrors happen, and I've got no part in those as to whether or not they happen. And it's not just at night; I think about going to the grocery store with my mom. What if I slap the stock boy? Or kick the manager because he doesn't have the correct cereal box? My point is that my mom doesn't know what might happen to me. So going insane is a big worry for me. That's the anxiety part of it all.

After Mom cleaned me up and Dad gave me my prescribed sleeping pill, they returned to bed to let me drift off, but I didn't fall asleep. I lay there empty and hollow inside, crying about how I've lost clients since I was in the hospital, and I can't get back into ethical hacking to the extent I was to save my life. The sadness overwhelms me to the point of physical aches and pains. I don't think the new antidepressant works as it should, but I have to remain on it for a few more weeks to see if it kicks in.

Sometimes it hurts to lift my arms. I'm just so exhausted from being sad. I stare at my mom and dad and watch their mouths move, but I can't hear anything. When I refocus, I forget the topic and my feelings regarding it. My headache hurts so bad that I've got to strain to move my head to turn over. My hands shake uncontrollably at times, usually when I'm alone, like at midnight, and I think about things in general. I contemplate the meaning of life and if I give a damn. I also ask myself whether I deserve Milo or friends in general

Last night, in the middle of the night, I thought back to yesterday's conversation with Milo. He seems to understand his depression. For him, he said, it revolves around a fear of not being enough. Not capable enough to work out in the woodshop, not a good enough student, not a good enough son or boyfriend, too weak to control his seizures, too stupid, and too indecisive, which we all know isn't the case.

Soraya gets similar feelings, too. She over worries that she's not good enough or has made too many mistakes to be worthy of love. Some days she doesn't show up to the group, and we have to go drag her out of bed because we know just how challenging lying in bed can be. It's the time when our feelings overwhelm us, and we try to win the game of life. Should I live, or should I die? Soraya started cutting. She says it was a downside of groups where she learned other bad coping tactics that make you feel better, but, in reality, are much worse.

Randy punches things. His parents hung a huge boxing bag in their basement, where he tries to take out his anger, which is a symptom of his depression. But sometimes, he doesn't make it there quickly enough and punches through the walls in his home. Last week, he hit a light pole in a grocery store parking lot and broke his hand in multiple places, including at the wrist. His poor emotional regulation and impulse control now result in profane outbursts at those nearby, in addition to damaging others' property. He's fighting an uphill battle personally and legally now.

On the other hand, Kerry suppresses his anger due to depression. He drinks his worry away, ending in loud outbursts of profanity and self-pity. He's angry at the world for how people treat him but doesn't realize he's digging his grave, health-wise, with his drinking to the point of alcohol poisoning, blackouts, and seizures.

And finally, with Ethan, it's similar to Kerry, but last week, we found him passed out with slow breathing. He was transferred to the hospital and diagnosed with Wernicke encephalopathy. He has impaired memory, vision irregularities, and loss of coordination which has prevented his discharge.

Both Randy and Soraya are creative writers working on novels where they create these awesome worlds so different from our own. Kerry has been working with Milo in the woodshop on his better days, and Ethan is an incredible fine artist who displays with his dad at local galleries. We're a band of misfits, but come together to pull each other up from what the public just sees as our doldrums and mistake us for stupid, lazy, and incompetent, which is far from the case.

We press on to prove ourselves and the public wrong, like now, as I sit stretching on my bedroom floor with my friend Violet as we prepare for a twenty-mile run from here in the suburbs into Minneapolis. While I've been thinking, Violet has rambled on about something I lacked the focus to care about, which is sad to say, but it's the truth. I don't worry about adolescent angst and petty disagreements as much as I did because of my larger problems and the necessity for solutions.

"Mia? Milo and Wyatt are down here waiting for you two young ladies," Dad yells from the bottom of the stairs.

"Be right down," I yell in response.

Violet and I, who are in better running condition, lead the way down the path along Purgatory Creek to Southwest Station. Using Valley View Road, we cut across to the paved trails at Bryant Lake Park, where we access Shady Oak Road up to the light rail trail. I don't know if Violet realizes how much we actually fell apart after that party. There were times I never wanted to see her again. So, as I run beside her, I'm constantly aware of that ever-present distance between us.

The light rail trail takes us into the city streets, where we dodge traffic, bicyclists, and pedestrians to get to the Mississippi River. There is the slightly curved Stone Arch Bridge, which is an old railroad crossing the river at St. Anthony Falls with its lock and dam, which is closer to the west end of the bridge.

We take our break and mosey along the bridge with other sightseers and tourists visiting the Mill Ruins to get that perfect picture to post on social media.

Upon returning from our run, we split off to our own homes to shower and ready ourselves for our double date, which will be dinner and a movie. The whole time at the restaurant, Wyatt and Violet talk like they're the only couple in the room. Milo and I don't mind, as we each don't like small talk or insignificant ramblings about who's dating whom in high school. When they get to the point of gossiping about a promiscuous letch of a person, I sit quietly, shocked at the audacity of their ignorance.

"You know, guys, that could easily be me that you're talking about," I open up the conversation.

"Oh, no, not you, Mia. This person we're talking about is nothing like you," Violet reaches for my hand, but I pull it off the table.

"Yeah, this person is like a sexual deviant. She sleeps with as many guys as she can get her hands on. It's nothing like what was forced on you," Wyatt adds.

I explain, "Promiscuity is often the result of sexual abuse or rape. The person starts to feel less of a person in their own eyes, and that of others, like you both who are incredibly judgmental of her, not knowing what she's endured in life."

"Okay, I'm sorry," Violet responds, but the look on her face is one of impunity.

Wyatt looks like a deer caught in headlights as he says, "Sorry, Mia."

When the silence overwhelms the table, I glance at Milo, who starts sharing projects he's started working on in his woodshop with Kerry. It's then I realize our trials and tribulations have distanced us incredibly from our former best friends who sit there listening to us like the young adults we've had to become to survive day to day with the weight of depression bearing down on us.

In the theater, Milo asks if he can hold my hand, and I let him. We sit there waiting for the feature while Violet and Wyatt try to toss popcorn in each other's mouths. Thankfully, the movie begins, the lights go down, and I'm holding hands with a guy who is safe and worthy of my trust. Afterward, while Wyatt and Violet wait in line to use the restrooms, Milo and I walk hand-in-hand out to my parents' SUV. We don't get in, though. Instead, we're slow dancing in the parking lot to music only we can hear.

Milo kisses my forehead, then I lean up to look into his eyes, and our mouths meet. At this time, there's no disassociation from my body like there has been up to this point. It's been slow but not as triggering as it could've been. Milo's been patient. There were days when his touch freaked me out, and I ran. But he understood, validated my trauma, and we waited until the self-doubt and shame lessened.

That's because he never downplayed my rape and listened intently without reacting or barging into my story. And on days when I told him I was overwhelmed by some of the negative associations, he respected me and never pressured me. I grow closer and closer to him each waking day as I allow him to touch me more frequently and intimately. This has empowered me to stand up and take the reins back from my rapist. Just because he took something valuable from me doesn't mean I can't reach out there, retrieve it, and watch it grow.

Mia

EPILOGUE

Everything is working out fine, but slowly. I'm still a white hat hacker, Milo is building and selling, and we're running daily while going to group once a week to see Randy, Kerry, Ethan, and Soraya there. She's got a new boyfriend who looks nothing like Milo. I'm relieved. I've been honest with myself about just how jealous I was of Soraya. But we've had an open dialogue that sometimes only we understand.

Milo and I plan on going to the U together, but living at home, not that there's anything wrong with that, because we know enough about ourselves to know that we need further stability to succeed for one more year.

AUTHORS' NOTES

Mental illnesses such as depression and anxiety aren't preventable. Unfortunately, most people don't have a fundamental understanding of mental disorders; therefore, they fear those experiencing a wound no one can see.

We need our society to continue bringing awareness to the mental illness issue that affects millions of Americans yearly, and to emphasize ensuring that those in need have access to proper care and treatment.

If you or anyone you know has been affected by mental illness or sexual violence, you can find help at the organizations below—understand that you're not alone in this struggle.

National Alliance on Mental Illness
<u>nami.org</u>
1-800-950-NAMI
info@nami.org

National Crisis Text Line
Text HOME to 741741

Active Minds
activeminds.org

988 Suicide & Crisis Lifeline
988lifeline.org
988 or 1-800-273-TALK (8255)

Mental Health America
mhanational.org

National Teen Dating Abuse Helpline
1-866-331-9474
www.loveisrespect.org

Rape, Abuse, and Incest National Hotline
1-800-656-HOPE
RAINN.org

National Domestic Violence Hotline
1-800-799-SAFE (7233) or 1-800-787-3224
www.thehotline.org

National Child Abuse Hotline
1-800-422-4453
ChildHelp.org

ABOUT THE AUTHORS

Angela Grey has created memorable, moving tales about the sometimes unexpected and challenging road to first love. Although Angela is a South Dakota native and an enrolled member of the Sisseton-Wahpeton Oyate, she's lived in Bensonhurst, Brooklyn, New York, on and off throughout her childhood. In her spare time, Angela enjoys budget travel, camping, grilling/BBQs with family, yoga, spirituality classes, and being a mental health advocate.

Website: angelagrey.com
Website: ShadyOakPress.com
Instagram: angelaellengrey
Facebook: angelaellengrey
Twitter: @AngelaEllenGrey

Paige Peterson received her bachelor's in psychology from the University of St. Thomas and an additional bachelor's from Rasmussen University. She resides in a Minneapolis suburb with her husband, dog, and two cats. She's a lover of coffee, all things travel-related, and camping alongside Lake Superior.